SPIRIT OF THE GAME

SPIRIT OF THE GAME

A ghost story about an outstanding soccer legend
- and the making of a new one!

Written by
Geoff Francis

(With additional material by Tony White.)

First Printing 2019

ISBN: 978-0-9964279-9-9

A **DRAWASSIC** book

www.drawastic.com

"FILMS I NEVER GOT TO MAKE":

Why did DRAWASSIC decide to publish a series of animated movie scripts that I have never made? Simple because, having struggled for a lifetime to get support for my filmmaking visions and meeting nothing but apathy and disinterest from the industry, I at least wanted to the public to have a chance to see what I say, to share a vision of animated filmmaking that is different to the mainstream and yet – I believe – has a valid voice in the world of entertainment filmmaking. The scripts published in this series are not all written by me but are certainly molded by what I was trying to achieve with animation – and they are certainly very different in style and approach. Once upon a time, when a certain Walt Disney has a unique vision and animation was pushed further and further towards imaginative storytelling and groundbreaking visual originality there was a chance to go beyond the formulaic and the predictable. Now all that has changed of course and despite my having made over 200 TV commercials (many award-winning), two TV Specials, several Short Films (one of which winning a BAFTA) and the title sequence for "The Pink Panther Strikes Again" movie, I have never been given a chance to show what I can do with a full-length movie venture – either in the mainstream or indie worlds. It is not as if my ideas were to out there and strange for modern audiences. Indeed, I challenge readers to deny that when reading the scripts I am publishing in this series of books. It's more the fact that the industry today has preconceived ideas of what audiences what, applying formulas of design, storytelling and subject matter that the industry, in its infinite wisdom, deems worthy of laying before modern audiences. It doesn't help too that with the advent of technology and the digital revolution the old-school notion of hand-drawn animation is no longer fashionable, unless of course is can be compromised and fashioned into what is deemed formulaic enough for the industry norms. I hope therefore in publishing these scripts readers will be able to make their own minds up on what is appealing to animation audiences and what is not. Remember however that all of these scripts are *"first-draft"* screenplays and have yet to go through the production mill that will enable many minds and many artistic

talents to form them into what might be an amazing animated experience. Nevertheless, I feel confident that the subject matter of each script will speak for itself and hint at what might have been, were there a little more vision, imagination and creative bravery in the industry they were designed for.

I thank you for giving this script a fair hearing in the court of public opinion!

Sincerely,

Tony White.

Concept Art introduction:

What you will see on the following pages is but the tip of an iceberg of things that have been created to push the development of this project forward. Even now we have not fully resolved entirely the style and the design look we would wish for the movie, were it ever to happen. Outside of the basic designs we have created, Tony White, has also single-handedly created two animated teasers that hint at what is to come and which would have hopefully gained the attention of investors. One of these was actually a short, animated tribute to the great Sir Stanley Matthews in memory of what would have been his 100th birthday.

So much more of the work that has been done in the past to try to get this project to the big screen can be seen on our "Spirit of the Game" website via the link below. However, in the meantime, it might help as you read this screenplay to visualize just some of the designs and creative processes we have gone through to the point where we now stand. In sharing it, we have to wholeheartedly thank all the artists* who have contributed to our journey – even though, as we say, we still haven't yet quite arrived at the final visual stages of where we wish the film to ultimately go. As groundbreaking as this story is, we believe that the artwork and the animation that must visually express it should be equally groundbreaking. That said, perhaps you will gain a hint of the kind of direction we are going for by viewing the various concept art pieces we have embraced thus far.

www.spiritofthegamemovie.com

* Creative talents who have helped us so far (and in no particular order) …

Peter Moehrle, Stephen Hanson, Thomas Liera, Fabrizio Pasini, David Boudreau, David Stoten, Wouter Tulp, Edit Sandor, Batka (Purevjav Batmyagmar), Gyorgy Tokodi, Maria Daines, Saille White, Carol Royle, James Bell, Patrick Robinson, Roger Martin, Jean Gough, William Key and Bad Animals sound services in Seattle.

STANLEY

Concept Art: SIR STAN

Concept Art: SIR STAN

Concept Art: STAN SKETCH

STAN

Concept Art: SIR STAN

Concept Art: SIR STAN

Concept Art: SIR STAN

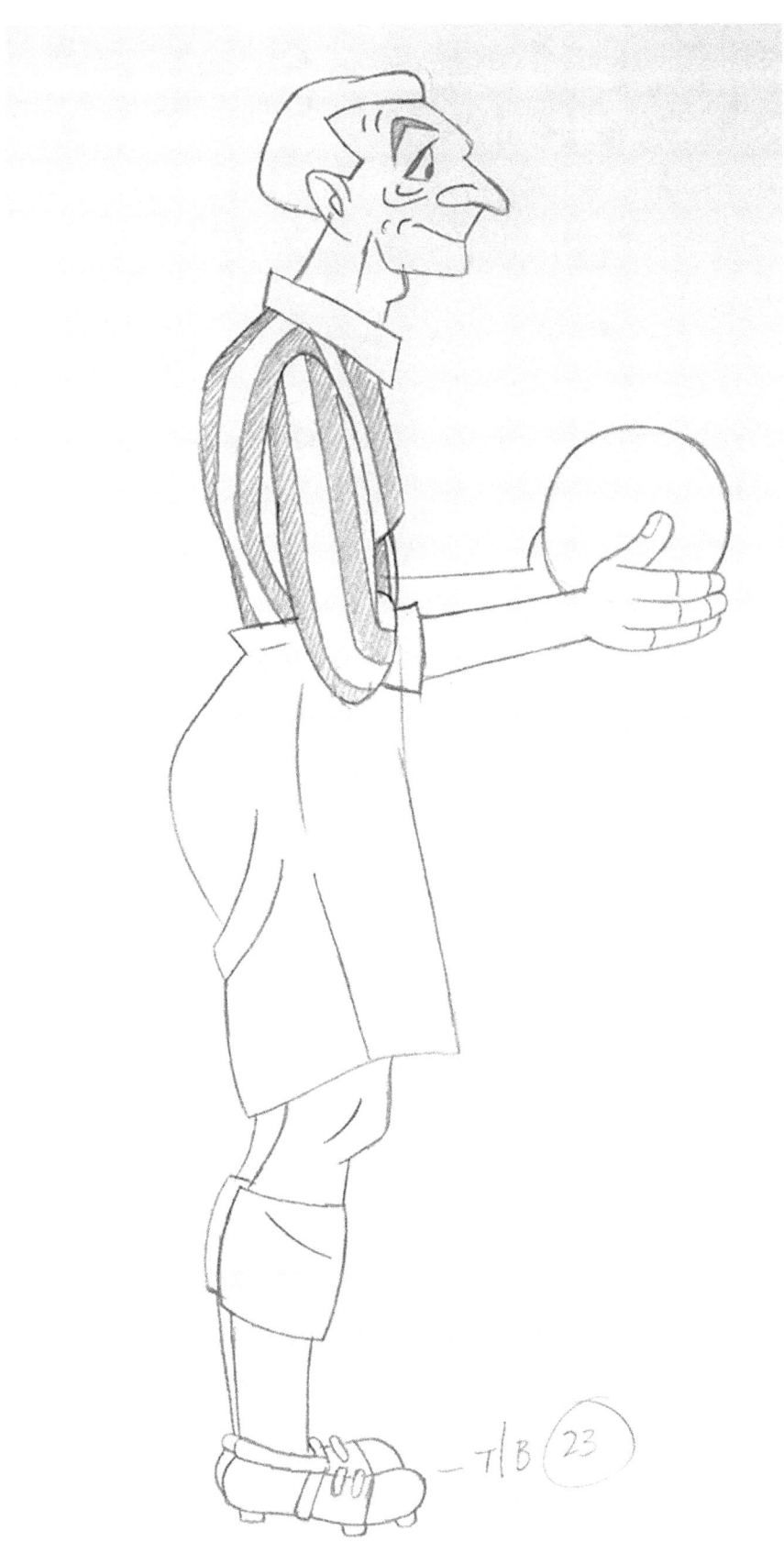

Concept Art: SIR STAN

Concept Art: MISCELLANEOUS

JAIME....

Concept Art: MATURE JAMIE

Concept Art: MISCELLANEOUS

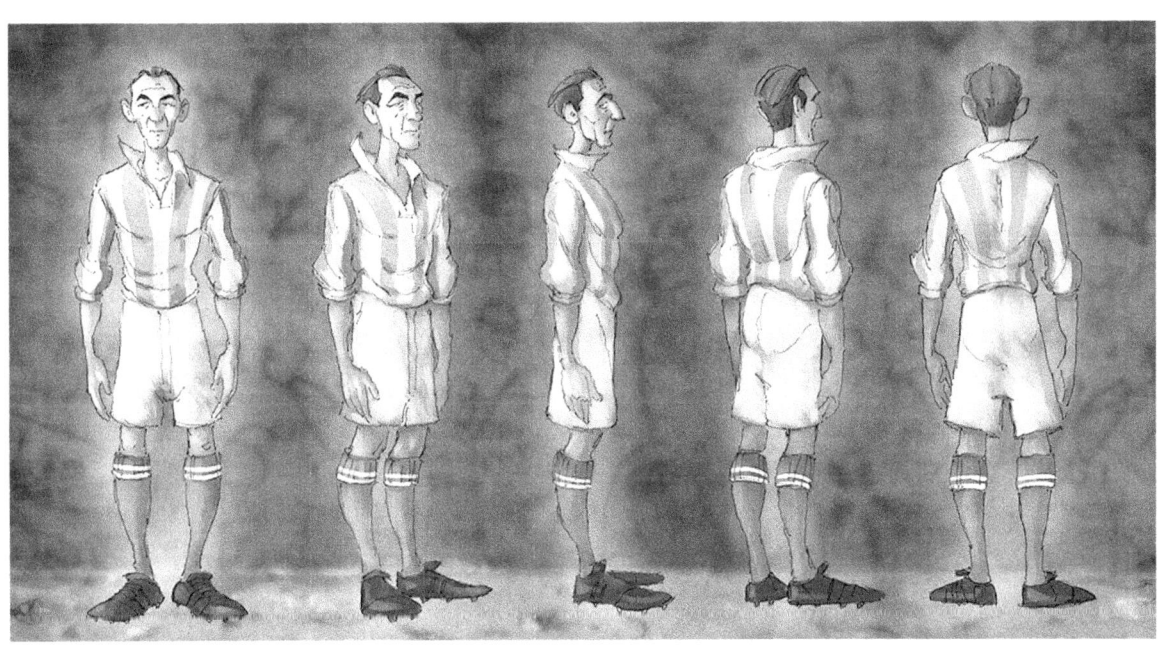

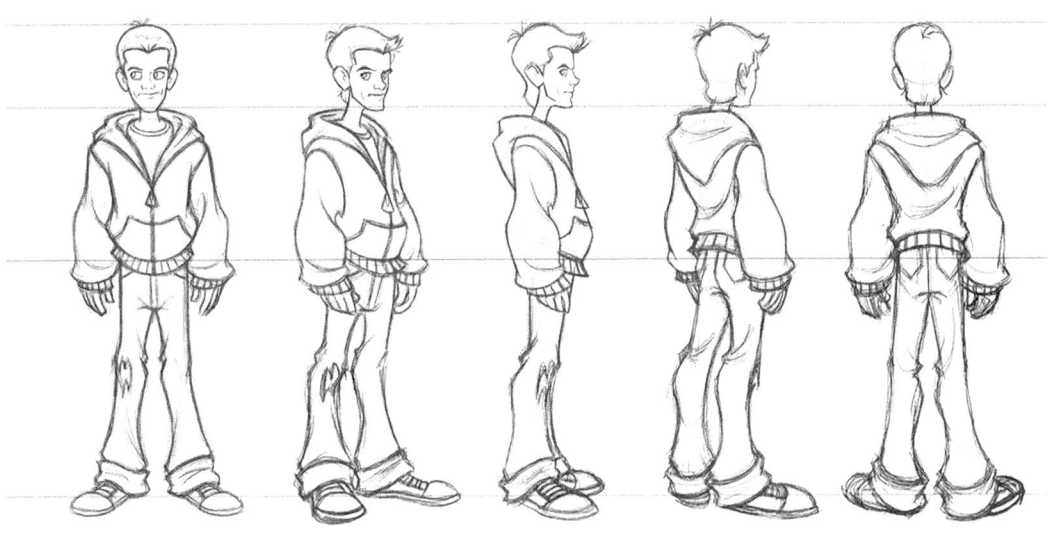

Concept Art: TURNAROUND MODEL SHEETS

Concept Art: STAN LAYOUTS

Concept Art: GRAPHIC NOVEL TEST

SPIRIT OF THE GAME ~ THE GRAPHIC NOVEL

Concept Art: GRAPHIC NOVEL TEST

Concept Art: BACKGROUND DESIGNS

SPIRIT OF THE GAME ~ THE GRAPHIC NOVEL

Concept Art: BACKGROUND DESIGNS

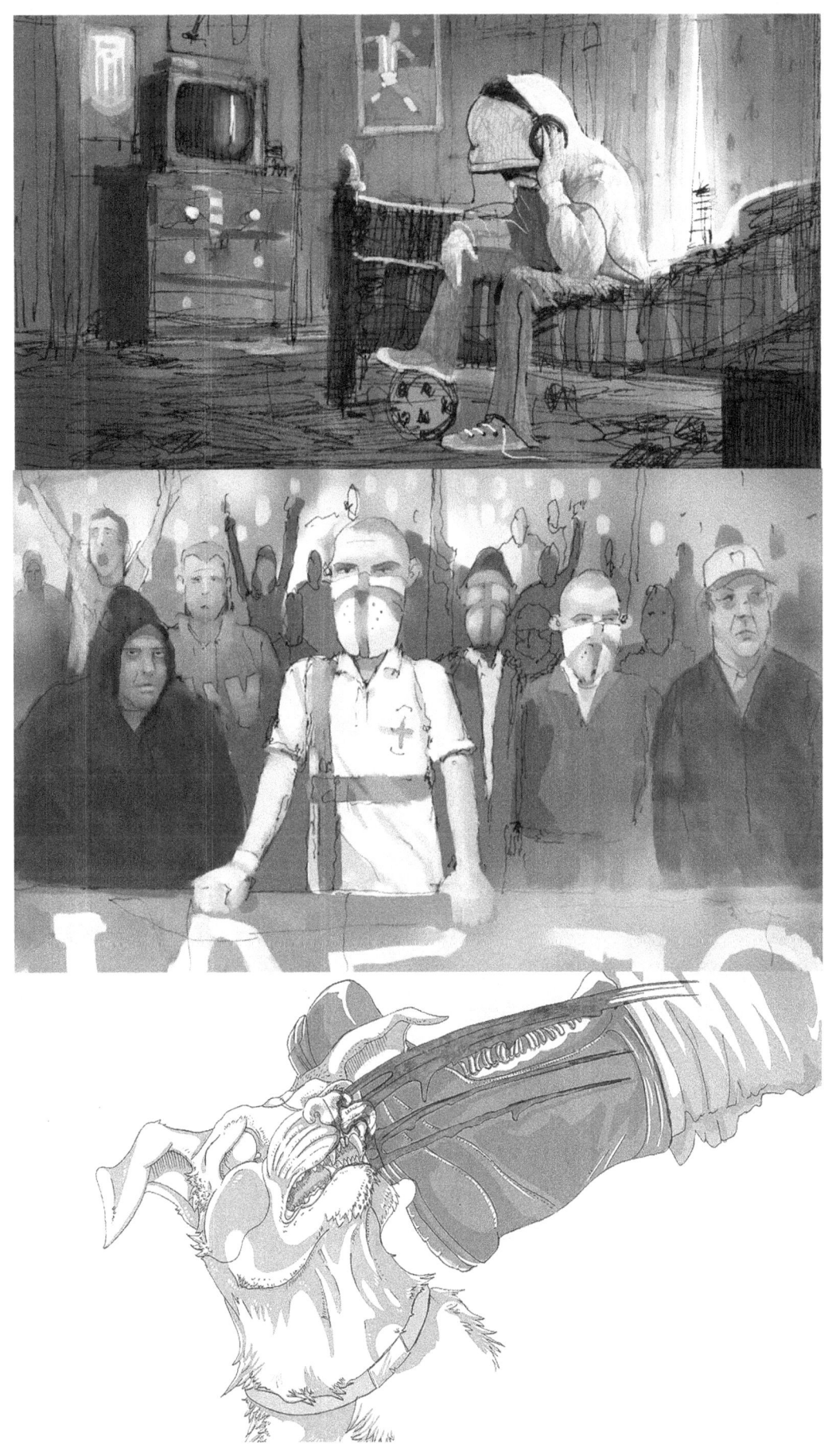

Concept Art: THE DARKER SIDE

The "method school" of animation: GETTING INTO THE PART!

Author / Producer introduction:

"Spirit of the Game" was originally conceived as a film script in 2000, in response to events in and around the game of football. It was a time when it seemed that the racism and hooliganism surrounding the game were particularly threatening and disruptive to more than the game itself. Racism can be seen as a white problem, cultivated in the young and more than often passed from generation to generation. This is where the heart of the story lies.

The script was intended to raise awareness of and challenge the thinking behind this behavior. Sadly, the significance of the issues addressed in the script increases year on year. In 2009, the story was released as a Young Adults' Novel, which then gave rise to a wonderful educational initiative, which in 2015 won endorsement, by the United Nations Department for Sport and Peace. Spirit of the Game has also been endorsed by the Stan Matthews' Foundation, Archbishop Desmond Tutu, Gordon Banks, the Society of Black Lawyers, Race for Sport, Joan Walley MP (Chair of the Cross Party Committee for Football) and Jeremy Corbyn MP, amongst others.

There had been a number of approaches to produce the film as a live action movie but it wasn't until BAFTA award-winning director Tony White shared his vision with me for a ground-breaking 2D animated film that I knew this would be the only way to realize the magic and grittiness of the tale in a way that would speak to all.

I would want to think I have lived my life in a way that takes no account of race, but even then never properly realized the real pain that racist attitudes have caused to so many. Whilst creating the story of Spirit of the Game and its many offshoots (film, book, audiobook, educational initiative, authorized biography of Sir Stanley Matthews and the associated BBC film of the same name) many good people have made me aware of just what it feels like to be the victim of racial attitudes and abuse.

I believe more than ever that this film deserves, nay, needs, to be made. Tony's vision for how it should be made will ensure it readily crosses borders with ease, so that its influence can be felt everywhere that people truly love the beautiful game and want it to fulfill its potential to bring the world together.

Geoff Francis

"**Spirit of the Game**"
Young Adults' Novel paperback edition available from most online retailers and to order from bookshops
 ISBN 978-1-907729-08-9

 Audiobook CD available from Amazon
 ISBN 978-1-907729-24-9
 Digital download available from most online audiobook retailers
 ISBN 978-1-907729-40-9

"**Stanley Matthews: Black Man with a White Face**"
Authorized biography available from most online retailers and to order from bookshops
 ISBN 978-1-907729-11-9

www.artistgeofffrancis.com

Director introduction:

"The ghost story of a soccer legend
~ and the birth of a new one!"

I have always love the movie, "It's a Wonderful Life", and have spent my entire career looking for its equivalent in animation. I never found it – at least until Geoff Francis introduced to me his "Spirit of the Game" story. I was immediately captivated by it and realized that my search was over!

I had always been a fan of the late, great soccer player, Sir Stanley Matthews. My memories of *"Sir Stan"* date back to when I was a child and my father would tell me stories of the great man, his achievements and his legacy. Stan was the supreme professional, an almost unrivalled sporting talent and, in view of the fact that he was still playing at the top level professionally at the age of 50, his longevity and legend will last forever. How wonderful therefore to discover a script that not only brought the great man back to animated life from my perspective, but also dealt with an issue that still remains as a cancer within the game – indeed the world – "racism".

My only significant contribution to the script - as I saw it ready-to-go from an animation perspective from the first reading - was that I felt that although aptly set around the time of the Millennium it needed to not only link with the modern game but also have some connection with the exciting development of soccer in the USA. The "MLS" was just emerging as a major force in the sporting arena in America at the time, so I felt some reflection of that at the beginning and end of Geoff's script was required. To my relief, Geoff enthusiastically agreed to what I scribed – hence the version of the script you are about to read.

I am sad that despite all the outreaching we have done, the unprompted accolades it received in and out of the sport and the increasing need for the subject matter to be addressed by the relevant powers that be, "Spirit of the Game" has never found a place in the film industry. I hope therefore by sharing this script with you now, you will at least sample in your mind what might have been – indeed, what still could be if someone, somewhere can share the same vision for the animated "Wonderful Life" that Geoff and I are proud to share. But now it is kick-off time for our story...

Tony White.

www.tonywhiteanimation.com

SPIRIT OF THE GAME

Written by

Geoff Francis

(With additional material by Tony White.)

AERIAL VIEW OF MAJOR US CITY IN NEAR FUTURE - NIGHT.

The camera travels as if an angel gazing down upon the earth. Distant lights from city speckle like stars below us.

                    VOICE
              (V.O. - MATURE JAMIE
                STEELE)
          They say when we die, we get to see
          everything we've done in our lives, right and
          wrong. Sometimes we can get the chance to
          see those things while we are still living. But
          that takes the intervention of someone quite
          extraordinary.

The camera starts to move downwards towards the city. The regular city lights are soon dominated by a more powerful light. It comes from a soccer stadium, with a game in play. As we now home in on the stadium we begin hear the distant chants of excited fans and the voices of two TV announcers who comment on the game as it reaches its breathtaking climax...

                    ANNOUNCER 1
          Although technically 'City'
          (placeholder name, final one to be
          determined later) have tactically controlled
          the midfield it is the 'Spurs' (placeholder
          name, final one to be determined later) who
          look most likely to score through Jamie
          Steele's breakaways. If anyone is able to win
          this match with a moment of genius, its him.

                    ANNOUNCER 2
          Yea Brian. Amazingly, its the American team
          that are showing the Europeans how the 'real'
          beautiful game should be played. But with
          only a couple of minutes of extra time left I
          guess its going to take the lottery of a penalty
          shoot-out to decide this one.

The camera continues to descend towards the stadium as fan chants and TV commentary grow louder.

                    ANNOUNCER 1
              (V.O.)
          Such a negative, defensive style City have
          brought to this one...
          relying solely on the occasional breakaway.
          Sterile, percentage football. The Spurs
          players, on the other hand, have been much

more creative. Steele's penetrating runs on the outside especially have brought the crowds to its feet. If only the forwards could have converted any of those brilliant crosses he's fed them with!

                    ANNOUNCER 2
                    (V.O.)
Yeah Brian. His first year in the MLS and he's brought the US game to the forefront of the world stage. Genius!

                    ANNOUNCER 1
                    (V.O.)
And today he's playing like a hot knife through butter John. No-one can handle that jinking winger's pace of his. If anyone's going to turn this game on its head in these dying seconds its Jamie Steele!

                    ANNOUNCER 2
Yep. And here he comes again!

The camera rapidly zooms down into the stadium light and the screen is momentarily filled with pure whiteness. It rapidly clears to reveal - ground level - Jamie jinking past a number of tired, leaden-footed City defenders, heading goalwards.
The clock in the corner of the screen shows that there are just a few seconds of extra time left. Jamie is showing incredible mastery.

                    ANNOUNCER 1
Look at that. Just like the great Stanley Matthews - no-one can stop him!

                    ANNOUNCER 2
Stanley who John?

                    ANNOUNCER 1
Long time ago in the British game John. Stanley Matthews was a legend...
                    (MORE)

                    ANNOUNCER 1 (CONT'D)
known as the 'Master of the dribble'. He was the best player in the world for his generation. Would probably still be the best today if the truth were known.

                    ANNOUNCER 2
Wow! Look at that Brian. He's almost free!

Jamie has now almost jinked his way into the penalty area with a good chance of a shot on goal. However, at the very last moment, a burly defender slides in and takes him down with crunching, two-footed tackle. Jamie sprawls on the grass, rolling painfully into the penalty area. The referee's whistle blows and the US fans bay for a penalty, Its a free kick, just outside the penalty area, but the big defender is shown a red card.

> ANNOUNCER 2 (CONT'D)
> Oh lordie! I felt that from here!

> ANNOUNCER 1
> Not penalty... but close. The ball's too close to goal to make it count though I'd say.

> ANNOUNCER 2
> Don't be too sure Brian. If he's up for it, Jamie Steele is quite capable of bending in from here!

> ANNOUNCER 1
> But maybe he's too injured to take it?

Jamie is definitely hurt. However, not one to play-act for the crowd or referee he calmly picks himself up, grabs the ball, rubs his battered and bruised legs and grimaces bravely goalward. His captain wants to take the ball from him but Jamie holds it tight, concealing his pain. The captain looks dubious, but relents. So Jamie proceeds to put the ball down where the tackle took place.

> ANNOUNCER 1 (CONT'D)
> Yep... he's going for it! Could this be the moment that makes soccer history? Remember, no American team has ever been in the World Club Cup final before, let alone win it!

Jamie looks to the excited, chanting fans behind the goal for inspiration. Then notices a lone and silent figure standing in front of them on the nearside of the fence.

CUT TO:

AREA OF THE CROWD BEHIND THE UNITED GOAL - SAME MOMENT.

The home team fans are chanting frantically.

> US TEAM FANS
> USA! USA! USA!

In front of them, the solitary figure Jamie has noticed stands watching him passively. He smiles. He is dressed in an old soccer kit and looks somewhat out of

place. We will soon learn that it is the great legend of the game, SIR STANLEY MATTHEWS.

CUT TO:

JAMIE CLOSE-UP - SAME MOMENT.

Jamie smiles back at Stan, as if seeing an old friend.

> MATURE JAMIE.
> (v.o.)
> I've never felt so much pressure as I did in that moment. What I was about to do could not only change my life but touch the lives of so many other people, including an entire sporting nation.

CUT TO:

WIDER SHOT OF THE GAME - SAME MOMENT.

The referee is pacing out the ten yards from the ball and sprays a line on the ground where the defensive wall needs to stand. The defensive wall adjusts itself grudgingly. At the same time, Jamie puts the ball down and adjusts it.

> ANNOUNCER 1
> Possibly the last kick of the game John. Could there be any more pressure on a player's shoulders than this!

> ANNOUNCER 2
> Talk about sorting the men out from the boys. This is probably the most important kick of Jamie's life and yet he looks as cool as a cucumber! Mind you, I wouldn't want to be in his shoes right now for all the tea in China!

As Jamie finishes adjusting the ball, everything suddenly goes into ultra slow motion. It is as if time itself is beginning to stand still. The fans' chants now become slow, distant and echoing. Jamie, poker faced, looks up at the goalkeeper. The goalie tries to second guess Jamie's thoughts by directing the positioning of the defensive wall, making it as difficult as possible for Jamie to get a clear shot in. Meanwhile Jamie takes a deep breath, slowly steps back from the ball and waits for the referee's whistle. He gives one last, lingering look to Stan, who gives him a look of encouragement and points to the corner of the goal where he wants Jamie to kick it.

CUT TO:

CLOSE UP OF JAMIE'S FACE - SAME MOMENT.

                    MATURE JAMIE.
               (v.o.)
          And so it all comes down to this. A single
          moment in time that will change my life, and
          touch the lives of so many others. When I
          think of where I came from, a punk kid with a
          huge chip on his shoulder, against the whole
          world.

The picture transitions to an earlier time and an earlier
place...

                                        FADE TO...

                    MATURE JAMIE. (CONT'D)
               (v.o.)
          At first I had really liked Amos but when he
          married my mum, and we had to move to
          Stoke to be with him, my ideas changed.

                                        CUT TO

EXT. PARK BENCH - EVENING

Headset still on, Jamie sits alone and withdrawn on a park bench. Suddenly a
football intrudes on his loneliness. A gang of youths gesticulate at him to kick the
ball back. He instinctively controls the ball, juggles it and impressively kicks it
right to their feet. They applaud and call him over. They are wearing blue and
yellow United shirts with 'Allen' & '9' on the back.

                                        CUT TO:

INT. FOOTBALL STADIUM - DAY

A game is in progress. Four lads aged 15/16, dressed in Allen shirts and draped
with England flags are among the crowd. Jamie is one, accompanied by PETER,
the youngest, intelligent but a born follower; JOE, a thin and wiry boy, afraid of no
one and a real head case; ringleader WILL, the eldest, a slightly overweight bully
boy. As the music stops, the boys chant for their hero MARK ALLEN.

                    BOYS
          Allen! Allen! Allen!

                                        CUT TO:

UNITED MANAGER - SAME MOMENT.

He shouts abuse in ALLEN'S direction.

                    UNITED MANAGER
          Allen, get stuck in. What the hell do you
          think you're doing? He's making a monkey
          of you.

                                                    CUT TO:

FOOTBALL PITCH - SAME MOMENT.

ALLEN takes the ball and heads up the wing. The black fullback on the home
team tackles him physically. As the fullback walks away ALLEN briefly makes an
ape gestures at him. The gang around Jamie make similar monkey noises and he
feels obliged to join in. The crowd turn on them.

                                                    CUT TO:

ALLEN's face reflects vengeance.

                                                    CUT TO:

FOOTBALL PITCH - SECONDS LATER.

Allen executes a particularly nasty foul which results in the same black player
taking a bad fall. As he lies injured on the ground ALLEN does his famous salute.
His young fans salute back to him. The referee rushes up and Allen stands
defiantly, hands on hips in a ridiculous manner to stare him down in a manic,
extremely intimidating way.

INT. FOOTBALL GROUND - SAME MOMENT.

The crowd sings singing the national anthem, while at the end of each line the
gang chants 'No Surrender'! Most members of the crowd look at them with
distaste, although some smile.

EXT. FOOTBALL GROUND - LATER

A post match fight is in heavy progress. JAMIE and THE GANG, adrenaline
running high, are in amongst the chaos. POLICE OFFICERS load up van's with
injured and angry thugs.

                                                    CUT TO:

INT. POLICE STATION, LEEDS - NIGHT

A seen-it-all white sergeant is interrogating (or attempting to) Jamie with AMOS defending him.

                    AMOS
          I grew up in South Africa under
          apartheid, I know what bad is (beat - the
                    eyes shift)
          and I know that boy doesn't have it in him,
               (beat)
          ...not deep down.
               (eyes shift again.)
          He's only fifteen years old, he's
          impressionable and...

                    SERGEA
          NT (wearily)
          Spare me the social psychology, I have to deal
          with the reality every day.

                    AMOS
          To me he is the reality.

Jamie looks embarrassed but maintains 'attitude'.

                    MATURE JAMIE.
               (v.o.)
          I had never been in a police station before
          and although I didn't show it I was really
          scared. I had no time for Amos then but
          something deep inside me grudgingly
          recognized the way he stood up for me. After
          all, I wasn't even his real son!

The SERGEANT searches AMOS' eyes, weighing him up.

                    SERGEANT
          Well Mr. Matkoni, I'll tell you what I'm going
          to do. I'm going to give that boy of yours...

Jamie's face reacts

                    JAMIE
          He ain't my dad. Blind, are you?

The sergeant looks fiercely at him.

                    SERGEANT (CONT'D)
          ...the benefit of the doubt and release
          him with a reprimand.

Jamie goes to speak but the Sergeant casts an eye in his direction and he thinks better of it.

> But... it will be on your cognisance. (beat) I
> don't want to see him in here again. OK?

                    AMOS
     Thank you sir.

Amos bundles Jamie out of the door.

                                        FADE OUT

INT. NIGHT CLUB - NIGHT

(Visual sequence only - seen as a grainy CCTV video.)

MARK ALLEN steps out of the gents, he rubs at his nose, sniffing hard. He notices the blonde girl and her mate, both a little worse for wear now are dancing on their own. Feeling cool he smugly makes his approach. Allen whispers something in her ear. The girl looks at her mate, they giggle.

Allen then looks smugly to the girl's friend and nods to his friends, offering them up as a choice for her. One of Allen's friends looks up, raises his glass to the girl. ALLEN turns his attention back to the blonde and whispers something more in her ear. She giggles again, squirming as Allen gropes at her and goes in for the kiss. She responds easily. The guys who are actually with the girls are returning to their spot with a round of drinks. One of them sees Allen moving in on his girl. He strides towards them purposefully, but Allen and the girl are to busy smooching to notice him. He grabs Allen's shoulder and spins him round. Allen sticks his face in the girl's boyfriend and stares him down, nose to nose. The girl just smiles stupidly. Her boyfriend flies at Mark landing him a good right hook. Allen stares at him in disbelief. He picks up a high bar stool and smashes it on the ground, picking up one of the legs he holds it out towards the man, flexing his shoulders as he does so. A black bouncer notices the commotion and speaking quickly into his walkie talkie wades into the trouble spot. As he grabs Allen and holds him back other security staff come in to assist.

EXT. STREET - NIGHT

AMOS drives as JAMIE sits in the back sulking. He looks out at the night life spilling out onto the streets as the clubs empty out. JAMIE Looks out the window, to the back of the car. Suitable MUSIC reflects the moods and feelings of participating characters.

                    MATURE JAMIE.
          (v.o.)
     I was always fascinated to see the way human

beings fill their time. Some work, some sleep
and some drink their lives away. I was never
a fan of the latter.

Amos interrupts Jamie's thoughts.

                    AMOS
          You alright, Jamie?

No reply.

                    AMOS (CONT'D)
          Lucky escape, hey?

AMOS notices Jamie momentarily glance at him in the rear view mirror - then
quickly looks away.

                    AMOS
               (CONT'D) (Sadly)
          OK, suit yourself.
                    (MORE)

                    AMOS (CONT'D)
               (then, suddenly distracted,
                pulling a phone out from
                his pocket)
          I'd better call your mum and let her know
          you're a free man!

Amos parks the car as he calls his wife. They stop outside a night club. At this
moment MARK ALLEN and his TEAM MATES are thrown out of the same club.
The bouncers return inside.
ALLEN stumbles into the car, his face contorted and pressed hard against the
windscreen. He glares in at AMOS.

                    ALL
          EN Black Bastard!
               (then to his friends)
          Get the nigger out. We'll show him whose
          country this is.

Jamie is thrilled to recognise his hero but scared, like a deer in the headlights, as
ALLEN drags AMOS from the car. The voice of Jamie's mum, CAROL, can be heard
on the phone which has fallen onto the front seat.

                    CAROL (V.O.)
          Hello?.... Amos?....

AMOS is pushed to the ground and the thugs start to kick him.

                                        CUT TO:

INT. CAROL'S FLAT - NIGHT

CAROL is standing in the middle of the room, the phone clutched to her ear.

                    CAROL
          Amos! .... What's going on?

Through the phone the sound of shouting and AMOS being beaten can be heard. In a state of hysteria she forces herself to disconnect, then dials 999

                    OPERATOR (V.O.)
          Emergency services.
                    CAROL
          Police...

EXT. STREET - NIGHT

ALLEN and his MATES are still laying into AMOS. JAMIE watches from the car, shocked but excited. He keeps looking down at the phone but can't bring himself to pick it up. The two GIRLS seen earlier in the club are among the on-lookers. Police sirens close. The blonde runs off and the thugs start to scatter leaving AMOS lying in the road, struggling for consciousness. Allen grabs the arm of the other girl. As the Saturday hero of the terraces runs past the car he glares at JAMIE full in the eyes. JAMIE stares back into eyes full of menace.

                    MATURE JAMIE.
                 (v.o.)
          It was like looking into the eyes of a
          trapped animal... it was terrifying to behold
          and yet somehow strangely exhilarating!

Instinctively Jamie does the Allen salute. The player returns it... then runs, dragging the screaming girl with him.

                                             FADE TO:

INT. HOSPITAL - NIGHT

JAMIE sits small and alone as people rush around him in the busy A&E department.

EXT. HOSPITAL - NIGHT

The police car pulls up. CAROL gets out and dashes into the hospital.

INT. HOSPITAL - NIGHT

JAMIE sees CAROL rush in and jumps up in relief.

                        JAMIE
            Mum.

She looks him over quickly relieved to see that he's not injured.

                        CAROL
            Are you okay?

                        JAMIE
            Yes, but...

                        CARO
                  L (Cutting in)
            Where's Amos?

                        JAMIE
            They've taken him to...

CAROL has rushed off to the reception desk.

                        CAROL
            I need to see Mr. Matkoni

                        NURSE
            I'm afraid only relatives...

                        CAROL
                  (Cutting her off)
            I am Mrs. Matkoni!

She looks the nurse squarely in the eye. The Nurse directs her to where AMOS is.
JAMIE watches sullenly from his seat. As CAROL rushes off JAMIE goes to follow
her. Then thinking better of it, he heads off towards the exit.

EXT. HOSPITAL

JAMIE sits on a bench in the hospital grounds his knees up to his chest.

                        MATURE JAMIE.
                  (v.o.)
            I was trying to make sense of it all. Allen
            was our hero but Amos had stuck his neck
            out for me. If it hadn't been for me he
            would never have been ended up in
            hospital.

Jamie crosses to the building and looks in through the windows. He watches a stretcher with AMOS on it being wheeled along. CAROL walks alongside. AMOS is lifted onto a bed and CAROL fusses around him, making him comfortable then settling herself into a chair. She is obviously intending to stay a while. A NURSE pulls the curtain behind the bed. Jamie appears confused and torn by all he has witnessed.

                                                    FADE

INT. CAROL'S FLAT

Jamie's bedroom is adorned by pictures of his football heroes, each with National Front haircuts. We recognise MARK ALLEN in a poster. JAMIE is playing music very loudly on his headset. CAROL enters.

                         CAROL
          Could you turn that off please?

                         JAMIE
                  (begrudgingly pulling
                  headset off his ears)
          Don't you like it? Rather I'd play Bob bloody
          Marley?

                         CAROL
          What you play in your own room is up to
          you.

                         JAMIE
          So what are you doing here then?

                         CAROL
          I want to talk about last night.

                         JAMIE
          You know what happened. I can't tell you
          anything the police haven't.

                         CAROL
          You didn't tell them anything
          anyway!

                         JAMIE
          Nothing to tell.

                         CAROL
          I think there is. I think you know who did this
                  (beat)
          Jamie... they're friends of yours aren't they?

JAMIE
In my dreams!

He puts the headset back on to cover his sense of guilt.

MATURE JAMIE.
(v.o.)
I didn't mean it like she heard it. But I wasn't
in a mood to explain.

FADE TO:

EXT. MULTISTORY CAR PARK - DAY

Top of a multi-storey car park. JAMIE is looking out over the urban sprawl and motor ways. Grey concrete and graffiti under grey skies. He and his friends pull on beer cans. When they have taken a couple of swigs an impromptu game of football commences with an empty can. Even with the can we can see JAMIE is a good player. He runs rings round the others giving a commentary as he plays.

JAMIE
And Allen swerves past one, past two and
smashes the ball past the helpless keeper
into the far corner.

JAMIE then assumes the inflammatory Allen posture and looks eagerly for peer approval. He gets it. They sit down and begin to talk.

WILL
So what are we going to do for money?

Shrugs all round.

PETER
My brother reckons there's this old bloke
who lives in Weggerton Street who's got
some good stuff... like really valuable...
stashed in his house.

WILL
Weggerton Street! That's a shit hole.
There can't be anything worth having
there.

JOE
It's got to be worth a try. What's to loose?

FADE TO:

EXT. WEGGERTON ST - NIGHT

Close up on front door. A boot kicks in the door and the boys rush in. JAMIE is pulled up short. The rugs on the floor are threadbare, there is a single bar electric fire, a Radio but no television. A single framed photograph of two men in RAF Uniforms is propped up on the mantelpiece. JAMIE has never seen a home with so little in it.

                    MATURE JAMIE.
          When I saw the place I felt bad. We had no
          right being there...

                    JAMIE
          I reckon Colin got it wrong, there's
          nothing here. Let's go!

The others ignore him.

                    WILL
          There's got to be something and if there
          isn't....

Will starts smashing at furniture and Joe follows obediently. JAMIE watches for a moment before picking up the photograph and studies it closer. WILL glares at him, wondering why he's not joined in too. Jamie complies by throwing the picture and breaking the glass. A voice comes from upstairs.

                    PETER (O.S.)
          Oi, Up here. I've found it!

They all dash upstairs.

INT. WEGGERTON ST BEDROOM

The BOY'S dash in to find PETER pulling two battered old cases out from under the bed.

                    PETER
          They're bloody heavy.

                    WILL
          Probably stuffed with notes.

                    PETER
          They're locked!

                    JOE
          I bet he's a old miser.

                    JAMIE
          Must be to live like this.

Suddenly the barking of an old dog is heard from downstairs.

                              ALL
                    (Whispered chorus)
          Shit!

PETER and WILL grab the cases and run.

INT. WEGGERTON STREET / STAIRS / HALL -- DAY

As they descend the stairs the dogs barking intensifies. But it is too old and
arthritic to climb them on its own. PETER jumps over the dog and out of the front
door followed by JOE. WILL who is in front of JAMIE puts the boot in. The dog lets
out a squeal of pain as Will disappears out of the door.

                              JAMI
                    E
                    (appalled)
          NO!

EXT. WEGGERTON ST - DAY

The Boy's scatter as an OLD MAN comes up the path. JOE & WILL give him a twist
and push him into a bush. JAMIE pauses and looks back at the senseless dog, torn
between helping it and escaping. The OLD MAN is disentangling himself from the
bush. JAMIE who knows he can't afford anymore trouble with the police runs off
unseen after the others.

EXT. WASTE GROUND - DAY

WILL, PETER and JOE have arrived first. They have broken the cases open and
the contents are being strewn everywhere.

                    MATURE JAMIE.
                    There was nothing there the gang were
                    interested in! (beat) Something told me
                    different.

                              WILL
                    Look at this shit.... This ain't fucking
                    treasure!

They turn on Peter.

                    WILL (CONT'D)
                    You're brother's a tosser, man! Come on,
                    There's nothing worth having here
                    anyway.

They all walk away, except Jamie. WILL chants, the others join in.

> ALL
> Allen for Engerland, Engerland! No surrender.
> No surrender.

JAMIE begins to return the strewn contents into the cases.

EXT. WEGGERTON ST - DAY

JAMIE approaches the open door tentatively. He has the two suitcases in his hands. He looks in. The OLD MAN, TOM is sitting at the foot of the stairs stroking the head of the whimpering dog. At first he doesn't see JAMIE.

> JAMIE
> (tremulously)
> Saw some boys running away from here.
> They dropped these.

TOM doesn't look up, his attention fully on the dog.

> TOM
> Oh... Yes... Thanks.

JAMIE puts the cases down and comes warily closer, scared of intruding but wanting to see what damage WILL has inflicted.

> JAMIE
> Will he be okay?

> TOM
> Don't know yet, son.

> JAMIE
> What about if we got a vet or
> something?

> TOM
> It'll just cause him more pain if we move
> him. He's quite old, you see.

> JAMIE
> Well can't the vet come here then?

> TOM
> I haven't got the money.

> JAMIE
> (Agitated, voice breaking) I
> know!

                    JAMIE (CONT'D)
          There's a herb thing my mum uses. She's a
          natural therapist you know. She gives it to me
          when I've been hurt. Half a mo...

He turns and runs out.

EXT. STREET - DAY

Jamie runs full pelt towards his home. (We see how fast and fit he is) He is half
glad to be physically free from the guilt of his involvement in the dog's suffering
and equally glad to be able to do something positive about it.

INT. WEGGERTON ST - DAY

JAMIE returns to Weggerton Street, breathless and with a small brown dropper
bottle in his hand. The dog is propped on a cushion. JAMIE proffers the bottle to
TOM who is slightly uncertain.

                    JAMIE
          It's okay. Its called 'Rescue Remedy'. Just
          herbs and things...
          and a bit of brandy.

                    TOM
                (Hesitatingly)
          Go on then.

                    JAMIE
          Me?

                    TOM
          It's your stuff.

JAMIE gently drops a couple of drops into the side of the dogs mouth. LADDIE
licks his lips. TOM casts his eye over the damage the gang has caused.

                    JAMIE
                (following   his   gaze   and
                suddenly   feeling   very
                guilty)
          I'll help you tidy up if you want.

                    TOM
          It isn't your problem.

                    JAMIE
          Yes it. I want to.
                (beat)

                    JAMIE (CONT'D)
Kitchen through here is it? I'll make you a
cup of tea then we'll make a start he?

                    TOM
Okay, lad.

TOM follows JAMIE with his eyes a possible respect forming, though he still
doesn't trust him.

                                        DISSOLVE TO:

INT. WEGGERTON ST - DAY

JAMIE and TOM are finishing tidying. LADDIE is on a chair with cushions
plumped around him. JAMIE is just about to put the photo of the two men in RAF
Uniform onto the mantelpiece. He stops to look at it.

                    TOM (O.S.)
Don't suppose you know who that is?

                    JAMIE
It's you, isn't it?

                    TOM
It is, but what about the other bloke?

                    JAMIE
                (Sarcastically)
Why is he famous?

                    TOM
IIe certainly is. Do you like
Football?

JAMIE nods. He smiles proudly.

                    JAMIE
I play for the District.

                    TOM
Yes?

                    JAMIE
Yea... a winger.

                    TOM
                (pointing to the man in the
                    picture)
That man, Stanley Matthews, was THE
greatest winger there ever was.

                        TOM (CONT'D)
          What if I told you he was the oldest man to
          play for his country at forty three. He won a
          European Cup Winners medal at thirty eight
          and didn't stop playing at the very top pro
          level until he was fifty!

                        JAMIE
          You're kidding me. My uncle Terry's not
          that age and he can't even run for a bus!
                    (beat)
          Was he your friend?

                        TOM
          My friend? Yes... and my boss. I was his
          driver.

Jamie looks again at the photograph. Behind him, unseen to them both, we
see the smiling figure of Stan watching.

                                                    FADE TO:

EXT. STREET - DAY

WILL, JOE and PETER hang out. JAMIE rounds the corner. WILL grabs him and
pushes him against a wall. The other's gather around menacingly.

                        WILL
          You bastard. You've grassed us up to that
          old git, haven't ya?

                        JAMIE
          No I haven't.

                        WILL
          Don't lie. Peter saw you go back with the stuff
          and you've been gone ages. We know cause
          we've been to your house.

JAMIE casts a sharp glance to PETER who lowers his eyes.

                        JAMIE
          Don't be stupid. If I'd grassed you up, don't
          you think the Police would have been round
          to see you all by now?

WILL is stumped. He pushes his face up close to JAMIE'S

                              WILL
                    You'd better not be lying.

He gestures, then slaps JAMIE for good measure.

                                                        FADE TO:

INT. WEGGERTON ST - DAY

Tom is feeding LADDIE small titbits by hand. The dog gently takes them.

                              TOM
                    You feeling a bit better, boy?

As he gets up a flicker of pain crosses his face. He steadies himself on the
arm of the chair and rubs at his heart.

                          TOM (CONT'D)
                    Might have a drop of your mum's stuff
                    myself you know.

He picks up the bottle of rescue remedy Jamie left on the table before and
takes a swig from the bottle.

                                                        FADE TO:

EXT. WEGGERTON ST - LATE AFTERNOON

PETER and JAMIE are passing a ball.

                              PETER
                    So why did you go back? I saw you...
                    and the cases.

                              JAMIE
                    Yeah so Will said!

                              PETER
                    Yeah...
                          (beat)
                    Sorry about that.

                          JAMIE S'alright.
                    Dunno really.
                          (beat)
                    I had to know if Laddie was alright.

                              PETER
                    Laddie?

The game stops. The lads take a break.

                    JAMIE
The dog.

                    PETER
Oh right.
          (beat)
But why did you take the stuff back?

                    JAMIE
Not sure. I just got the feeling it was special.
His whole life was in them cases. Stuff he'd
collected all his life. About this bloke called...
          (tuts)
Shit, can't think what he said his name was
now.

                    PETER
          (more seriously)
You wanna stop winding Will up. He thought
you'd found something worth money in the
cases.

                    JAMIE
Will's a shit stirring bastard. (beat)
Come on it's getting dark. I've gotta get
home.

They leave the Waste Ground and start walking home.

EXT. WASTE GROUND - LATE AFTERNOON

JAMIE and PETER continue on up the bank.

                    PETER
So what's so cool about this bloke in the
suitcase? Was he famous?

                    JAMIE
Yeah. He won everything and not just
when he was young. He was still playing
at fifty!

                    PETER
No way!

                    JAMIE
Straight up! That's what Tom said.

                    PETER
Who's Tom?

                    JAMIE
The old bloke.

                    PETER
He's gotta be having you on or he's going
senile.

                    JAMIE
I don't think so. That's the sort of stuff that
was in the cases. Cuttings and things. Said he
played for England when he was forty three.

                    PETER
Bullshit. Even if it's half true he must have
been some sort of super hero.

EXT. STOKE CITY GROUND - LATE AFTERNOON

The Statue depicting the three ages of Stan in motion Stands eerily in the fading
light as the boys approach the summit of the bank.

                    JAMIE
        Over there, those statues. That's him!

They look up at the statue. We see them looking in wonder from the statue's
POV. Again, unseen by them both, Stan's ghost stands in the background,
watching them.

                                                    FADE TO:

INT. CAROL'S FLAT/HALL

JAMIE enters

                    JAMIE
        It's only me. Mum?

JAMIE turns on the light and picks up a copy of the local evening paper lying on
the door mat. On the front cover is a picture of MARK ALLEN doing his famous
salute on the pitch, and a headline that reads. 'Allen England's weapon of Mass
destruction?'.

CAROL comes out into the hall.

                    CAROL
        That today's paper?

He instinctively puts the paper behind his back as he flashes back to ALLEN and his thugs pulling Amos out of the car.

> JAMIE
> (Unsure and uncomfortable) Nah,
> it's an old one, Peter gave me, it's got
> some stuff on Mark Allen, that's all.

> CAROL
> OK. I'm back to the hospital. I've left you
> some dinner on the counter.

She kisses JAMIE on the cheek as she passes him.

FADE TO:

EXT. WEGGERTON ST - DAY

TOM opens the door to JAMIE.

> JAMIE
> I wondered how Laddie was?

> TOM
> He's improving. Would you like to see him?

JAMIE nods.

INT. WEGGERTON ST - DAY

JAMIE follows TOM into the sitting room. LADDIE looks up from his place on the settee and wags his tail.

> TOM
> I was wondering if we'd see you again.

JAMIE pauses for a second but doesn't respond. He sits next to LADDIE and strokes his head. He does not raise his eyes to engage TOM. After a while he does.

> JAMIE
> You know that stuff you were telling
> me about... what's his name.....

> TOM
> Stan... Matthews?

> JAMIE
> Yeah that's it, Stan.

                    TOM
Yes.

                    JAMIE
Well, was it really true?

                    TOM
Why shouldn't it be?

                    JAMIE
It's just I was telling one of my mates, and he
couldn't get his head around it all.

                    TOM
                (half to himself)
I expect there are a lot of things your friends
can't get their heads around.

JAMIE looks at him quizzically, uncertain of where this last remark was coming
from. He pauses.

                    JAMIE
Well, is it all true?

                    TOM
                (Impatiently)
Of course it's true.

JAMIE waits for TOM to continue. But he doesn't.

                    JAMIE
Could you tell me more?

                    TOM
You really want to know?

                    JAMIE
I really want to know.

                     T
                OM
                (Smiling)
Okay.

TOM goes to the hallway and unhooks an old mac from the stairs. He puts
it on and pulls out an old cap from the pocket, he gestures with it.

                    TOM
Come on then.

JAMIE gets up patting LADDIE as he goes.

EXT. SEYMOUR ST - DAY

Camera picks up the plaque on the front of the house.

'Sir Stanley Matthews was born here 1st April 1915. Footballer and gentleman'

>TOM
>Footballer and Gentleman.

>JAMIE
>What's that about then...
>'Gentleman'?

>TOM
>Well, firstly he was a gentle man...

>JAMIE
>Soft, you mean?

>TOM
>No! Look... you think it was soft in those days
>do you? How soft do you think you need to be
>to last at the top of your profession for thirty
>five years?

JAMIE remains quiet.

>TOM (CONT'D)
>He was gentle in the kind way he dealt with
>people. He had time for everyone. And... he
>remembered things about them. Made them
>feel special. He had integrity.

JAMIE shrugs

>TOM (CONT'D)
>He acted on what he believed.
>Played by the rules.

>JAMIE
>Rules are for fools. Mark Allen doesn't bow to
>anyone and look what he's got.

>TOM
>You want to be like him?

                    JAMIE
Doesn't everyone?

Tom shrugs

                    JAMIE (CONT'D)
Well, not you. Not older people.
Your time's gone.

                    TOM
Thanks!

                    JAMIE
You know what I mean. You've got to grab
what you can these days.

                    TOM
And look what that's done to the world!

                    JAMIE
Yeah, save the planet. I learn that stuff in
school. But that's all 'cause what older people
have done. They've had theirs. We want ours
now.

                    TOM
The earth's not big enough for the insecure
greed of the Mark Allen's of this world, trust
me... with their multiple sports cars and all
the rest.
        (then tetchily)
Anyway, I thought you wanted to know
about Stan?

                    JAMIE
I do.

                    TOM
Well lets move on, eh.

EXT. WELLINGTON RD. SCHOOL - DAY

JAMIE and TOM approach Wellington Road School.

                    TOM
This is where Stan went to school.

TOM leads the way across the school playground to the door

                    TOM (CONT'D)
He was the most perfectly balanced player

of all time, and his sudden bursts of speed
over twenty yards or so was one of the
delights of the game.
      (chuckling at the memory) They
called him 'The Wizard of Dribble'.

TOM stops at the door looking round for JAMIE. TOM shuffles in, obviously a regular. JAMIE takes a quick look around before following.

INT. WELLINGTON RD. SCHOOL

TOM and JAMIE gaze up at the stained glass window erected in memory of Stanley Matthews.

                JAMIE
Wow!

EXT. STREET ABOVE CITY - DAY

JAMIE and TOM sit on a bus as it trundles above the city and past a house.

                TOM
            (Points out a house)
That was Stan's last house. Sadly Mila, Stan's
second wife, died there from a sudden heart
attack...
and six months later Stan was dead too.

                JAMIE
What did he die of?

                TOM
A broken heart son, a broken heart!

EXT. VICTORIA GROUND - DAY

The original Victoria Ground is now wasteland and JAMIE is fully engrossed in TOM'S stories of Stan. He looks at the ground. We hear the echoes of the chanting of Stanley's name.

                TOM
Hard to believe this was a football pitch, but it
was... the Victoria Ground. Stoke were near
the bottom of the Second Division when Stan
went back to them in nineteen sixty one. The
team was transformed and attendances rose
from nine thousand to thirty six thousand.

The following year they were promoted and
Stan scored the winning goal that took them
up.

Some BOYS are playing football with a makeshift goal made from bricks and
a plank of wood.

                    TOM (V.O.) (CONT'D) This is
          also where Stan played his
          last game in professional football. What a
          glorious night. The world came to see and the
          greatest players from more than one
          generation made it there.
                    (voice breaking)
          You could see the tears in his eyes as they
          carried him off on their shoulders.

The boys' ball falls at Jamie's feet. He returns it...
perfectly weighted to land on the head of the BOY who is standing at the pile
of bricks which is the far post. He nods it down into the goal and signals
thumbs up to JAMIE.

                    TOM (CONT'D)
          Bet you couldn't do that again.

                    JAMIE
              (confidently)
          I wouldn't if I were you.

TOM smiles, then rubs his chest.

                    TOM
          Think I should be getting back to
          Laddie

                                        FADE TO:

INT. WEGGERTON ST - DAY

JAMIE is sitting on the settee stroking LADDIE. TOM is sitting on the other side
of the fire place in an arm chair.

                    JAMIE
          He seems a lot better.

                    TOM
          Fingers crossed, eh?

He crosses his fingers. Jamie holds his crossed fingers up too,

>   TOM (CONT'D)
>   He didn't deserve what happened.

>   JAMIE
>   That Will's a bloody nutter... I...

JAMIE pulls himself up short realising that he's just given himself away.

>   TO
>   M It's okay, son.
>   (beat)
>   You didn't think I didn't recognise you when
>   you bought the cases back, did you?

Jamie's ashamed. TOM goes towards the mantelpiece and starts poking about in a pot.

>   TOM (CONT'D)
>   I've something here I want you to have.
>   (beat)
>   Might not seem much, but to me it's very
>   special.

Finds what he's looking for.

>   TOM (CONT'D)

>   Ah, there it is.

He pulls a small round badge with a black and white image on it out of the jar.

>   TOM (CONT'D)
>   When people used to write to Stan he would
>   always reply personally...
>   and with the reply he'd send one of these
>   badges he'd had made up.

He hands the badge to JAMIE who is not impressed. Badges are not cool.

>   JAMIE
>   Oh, mmm... thanks.

>   TOM
>   About six weeks after his wife died, he asked
>   me to take him to the airport. Jean, his
>   daughter, and Bob were taking him away for
>   a break to Spain. He'd been sorting through
>   stuff in the house and tucked in the corner
>   of a drawer he'd found this badge. The very
>   last one. I don't know why but as we said

goodbye at the airport he pressed it into my
hand.
            (beat... with earnestness) And
now I want you to have it.

                    JAMI
            E (uncertain)
No. It's yours. It's special to you.

                    TOM
I really want you to have it. (beat)
It may not look much special but it really is.
You see, he died just after he gave it to me.
Please?

                    JAMIE
            (embarrassed)
Thanks.

He slips it in his pocket.

                                        FADE TO:

EXT. SCHOOL FOOTBALL PITCH - DAY

JAMIE in action, showing how good he is. On the touchline are FATHER'S of the
team in which he plays. PETER and WILL are also in the team. PETER isn't a bad
player but a little too delicate for this sort of game. WILL is a bit of a clogger.
Tom watches too. STAN's ghost also... a little behind the shoulder of Tom.

                                        CUT TO:

C/UP ON TOM'S FACE.

                    TOM
            (to himself)
Hmmm? He's good Stan!

Unseen by Tom, ghost STAN nods in acknowledgement.

                                        CUT TO:

SCHOOL FOOTBALL PITCH - SAME MOMENT.

JAMIE executes a particularly neat move. The FATHER'S of some of the other lads
cheer from the touchline. They are rough, ready and beer bellied. Their sons are
being encouraged to mete out rough treatment to two ASIAN LADS in the
opposing team. This spills out into overt racial abuse. WILL is red carded for a

really nasty tackle. Threats of violence are made to the REF. There's a lot of posturing towards the FATHER and UNCLE of one of the ASIAN BOYS. When they stand up to him, Wills father turns on his own father. Then clouts his son.

                                                                    CUT TO:

EXT. SCHOOL CHANGING ROOMS - DAY

JAMIE who knows he's played well, emerges and walks towards TOM with a smile on his face.

                         JAMIE
              Well? What do you think?

                         TO
              M I'm impressed.
                    (his smile fades)
              And disappointed. You're too good a player
              to play like a thug!

                         JAMI
              E (puzzled)
              What do you mean?

                         TOM
              Stan was never ever warned by a referee,
              never mind carded... in thirty five years...
              and despite lots of provocation!

JAMIE looks round. He sees the OTHER BOYS with their FATHERS heading for their cars.

                         JAMIE
              I have to go.

                         TOM
              Okay, son.

JAMIE jumps into Will's dad's van, then looks back at TOM, who stares back, nodding.

                                                                    CUT TO:

INT. WILL'S FATHER'S VAN

Will's father is passing around cans of beer laced with white powder to the boys. JAMIE takes his but doesn't drink.

                    WILL'S FATHER:
So what's it like having a black man for a
dad, eh?

                    JAMIE:
He's not my dad.

                    WILL'S FATHER : Well,
he sleeps with your mum.
            (smirks to his dad.) She's a bit of
a witch I hear.
Believes in herbs, 'black' magic and
things.

                    JAMIE:

What?

                    WILL'S
                    GRANDFATHER: (to his son,
                    ignoring Jamie)
Bet it's a noisy place that bedroom of theirs!

                    WILL'S FATHER;
Would be if I were there! Lovely piece of
arse that mum of yours. I'd give her one
given half a chance!

                    WILL'S GRANDFATHER:
What, even after a black man's been
there?

They laugh drunkenly. Jamie fumes his can. He puts it aside and stares out of
the van window sulkily.

                    MATURE JAMIE.
            (v.o.)
I didn't like what they said about my mum of
course, but I was too scared to stand up to
them at the time. But I think it was then I
began to realize I had absolutely nothing in
common with any of them, 'specially Will!

                                                        FADE TO:

INT. CAROL'S FLAT - NIGHT

Jamie looks down the corridor towards his mother's bedroom door. His face
confused. He enters his own bedroom and closes door. Loud music.

INT. TELEPHONE BOX - EVENING

TOM talks into the phone. Stan's ghost lingers outside.

                    TOM
          Bob, I'd like someone to have a look at
          this boy. There's something of Stan
          about him.
                    (then, rubbing chest)
          But it needs to be soon I'm afraid. (beat)
          Thanks Bob. You won't be sorry.

                                        FADE TO BLACK:

EXT. GRAVEYARD - DAY

A crowd of faces stand around the grave. JAMIE fights to hold back the tears.
Earth falls onto a coffin and a pious vicar says "ashes to ashes, dust to dust", etc.
The wreath on top tells us that TOM is the one in the coffin... but we can tell also
as the ghosts of Stan and Tom are standing watching the proceedings. JAMIE
fondles the badge and looks at it from time to time. As the MOURNERS disperse a
homely middle-aged woman comes across to JAMIE. Stan and Tom remain to
observe.

                    WOMAN
          You must be Jamie.

JAMIE nods, but dare not speak. He doesn't want to cry.

                    WOMAN (CONT'D)
          Dad told me all about you.
                    (beat)
          He left some things he wanted you to have.

                    JAMIE
                    (voice breaking)
          I don't want anything.

The WOMAN puts a comforting hand on his shoulder.

                    WOMAN
          Please. Come round to his house
          tomorrow
                    (beat)
          Please?

JAMIE nods.

>   WOMAN (CONT'D)
>   Good.
>   (beat)
>   And thanks for coming today, it would have
>   meant the world to him.

Jamie nods again and turns away wiping his nose on his sleeve. Tom turns to Stan.

>   TOM
>   I've done what I can Stan. Now its over to
>   you!

>   FADE TO BLACK:

INT. WEGGERTON ST - DAY

Most of TOM'S meager possessions have gone. The two suitcases are sitting in the middle of the floor. The WOMAN and a MAN of similar age are shifting the rest out into a beaten up old van. The woman stops to talk with JAMIE.

>   WOMAN
>   He wanted you to have these.

She gestures to Tom's cases.

>   WOMAN (CONT'D)
>   God knows what you'll do with them, but I
>   guess he thought you'd appreciate them.

JAMIE is taken aback, then picks them up.

>   JAMIE
>   Thanks.

He Picks up the cases and begins to walk. Then he stops, turns and blurts out...

>   JAMIE (CONT'D)
>   What's going to happen to Laddie?

>   WOMAN
>   Oh, he's coming with us
>   (beat)
>   Unless you want him?

                         JAMIE
Really?

                         WOMAN
Why not. We're both at work all day.
You'd better ask your mum first though.

She finds a pencil and paper and writes down a phone number, hands it to
JAMIE.

                     WOMAN (CONT'D)
This is my number you can come and get
him tomorrow if you like.

JAMIE exits more cheerfully, a little bit of hope rising.

                                                      FADE TO:

INT. CAROL'S FLAT - DAY

JAMIE has asked CAROL if he can have Laddie.

                         JAMIE
Can we. Pleeeaaassseee?

                         CAROL
               (voice raised)
Jamie, we live in a flat. It's no place for a
dog. Laddie's much better off where he is.

                         JAMIE
How do you know that? She doesn't really
want him.

                         CAROL
               (softening with the look in
                Jamie's eyes)

                     CAROL (CONT'D)
I'll tell you what, when Amos gets out of
hospital we'll talk again. Okay?

                         JAMIE
Amos! What's it to do with him? Tom was
my friend. Laddie is my friend!
               (begins to cry)
What does Amos care!

                         CAROL
He cares!

                              JAMIE
                    Crap!

JAMIE storms out of the kitchen. CAROL sits at the table tears forming as
she hears his bedroom door slam and an inevitable music is turned to
maximum volume.

INT. CAROL'S FLAT - DAY

JAMIE sits on the bed upset and stroppy.

                              JAMI
                    E (To himself)
                    Screw Amos! He's not on his own, with no-
                    one giving a shit!

The tears roll. His eyes stray to the cases. He pulls one onto the bed and begins to
look through its contents. He fondles the fragile old papers. Suddenly he spots a
photograph of the 1938 England Team in Berlin giving the Nazi salute.

Through his tears he scrutinizes the photograph.

                         JAMIE (CONT'D)
                    (to himself)
                    It's him. I guess he hated blacks too. Sorry
                    Tom but Stan was one of us after all.

Off camera, a soft firm voice in a Stoke accent.

                              STAN
                    (o.s.)
                    No. You've got it wrong lad.

JAMIE turns to see the ghost of Stan behind him.

                              JAMIE
                    (shocked out of his tears) Stan?

JAMIE backs away but Stan bids him its OK.

                              STAN
                    The only reason we gave that salute was
                    because we were ordered to. We didn't
                    believe in Nazism... and nor would you if you
                    really knew what it means! It releases hate in
                    people who didn't even know they had it in
                    them.

                                        FADE TO BLACK.

INT. CAROL'S FLAT/JAMIE'S BEDROOM - DAY

Jamie is lying on his bead staring when, suddenly there is a noise at the window. JAMIE jumps out of his skin. He look out. Below WILL, PETER and JOE are throwing stones up at the glass. They see JAMIE looking down at them.

                    WILL
          Oi, You coming or what?

                    JAMIE
          What?

He opens the window.

                    WILL
          You coming?

                    JAMIE
          Where?

                    WILL
          The match, you twat!

                    JAMIE

              (almost reluctantly)
          Yeah. Hang on.

EXT. STREET - DAY

JAMIE joins the others who are propping up various walls. WILL puts his arm forcibly around Jamie's shoulder, more controlling than comforting and marches him off. The others follow.

EXT. FOOTBALL GROUND - DAY

The boys arrive for a youth cup match. They pass a lad holding out some black and white wrist bands under a banner announcing 'Kick Racism Out of Football'. JOE and PETER hold the boys arms down while WILL stuffs the wrist band in his mouth. JAMIE, now struggling hard to fit in, fakely joins in the laughing as they enter the ground.

EXT. FOOTBALL GROUND - DAY

THE GANG hassle the black and Asian players and on-lookers. JAMIE carefully scrutinized by WILL and JOE is pushed to the forefront of the taunting.

                                                        FADE TO:

INT. CAROL'S FLAT - DAY

CAROL is in the kitchen cooking. She hears the door slam.

                    CAROL
          That you love?

                    JAMIE (V.O.)
          Yeah.

JAMIE walks in sniffing the air.

                    JAMIE
          Something smells good.

CAROL notices JAMIE is not wearing his usual football colours.

                    CAROL
          I thought you were a United fan?

                    JAMIE
          I am.

                    CAROL
          But aren't they blue and yellow?

JAMIE grins back sheepishly.

                    JAMIE
          I'm starving!

                    CAROL
          Get one of my special pizza's out of the
          freezer and I'll heat it up for you.
                    (gestures to the part
                    cooked food)
          This is for tomorrow. I thought we'd have
          a family celebration.

                    JAMIE
          Family? Is Dad coming?

                    CAROL
          Yes. The specialist rang this afternoon and
          he said Amos is definitely on the mend and
          he can come home tomorrow! Isn't that
          great?

CAROL beams. JAMIE is pissed off.

                    JAMIE
Yeah. Great.

                    CAROL
I thought you'd be pleased?

                    JAMIE
Pleased! You've replaced my real dad with
a fucking darkie! When are you gonna get
it through your head that Amos never has
been and never will be my 'dad'!

CAROL slaps him hard around the face. JAMIE stares at her in angry defiance.

                    CAROL
(Shocked, she's never hit her son before.)
Oh God. I'm sorry it's just... I just don't
understand what's happening to you.

                    JAMIE
You and him! That's what's happening to
me. Why did you have to marry him?

                    CAR
       OL
       (Stunned)
I love him.
       (beat)

                    CAROL (CONT'D)
And he loves me. You can understand that
can't you, love?

                    JAMIE
       (angrily ignoring the
        question)
Do you know what everyone says
about you?

                    CAROL
By everyone I assume you mean those misfits
you hang out with at the football.

                    JAMIE
The only misfit round here is you and
Amos!

JAMIE storms back out of the house.

                                        FADE TO:

EXT. STREET - DAY

JAMIE runs not caring where he's going. STAN is standing outside a shop, as JAMIE turns a corner and runs through him. A sudden chill stops him in his tracks. He turns...

                    JAMIE
          Are you really... for real?

                    STAN
          As real as you Jamie.

                    JAMIE
          No, I mean... you're dead! (beat)
          Aren't you?

                    STAN
          Now that's an interesting one. I guess
          technically I'm dead, but as you can see I'm
          not gone.

                    JAMIE
          But why aren't you?

                    STAN
               (laughs, changing the
                subject)
          This is where my father's barber shop
          used to be.

                    STAN (CONT'D)
          They called him the fighting Barber of Hanley,
          on account of his being a boxer as well. He
          taught me a lot.

                    JAMIE
               (Stunned, starts babbling)
          My dad travels the world with Rock Bands.
          He's pretty cool.

                    STAN
          Musician is he?

                    JAMIE
          No, he's a roadie.

                    STAN
          What does that mean?

                    JAMIE
He sets up the equipment.

                    STAN
Oh.

                    JAMIE
But he's a good one, he does it for a lot of big
bands.

                    STAN
So I expect you get lots of free tickets for
concerts then?

                    JAMIE (realisation
            dawning)
No! I don't get any.

                    STAN
What?

                    JAMIE
No. I can't even remember...
            (beat)
...when I last saw him.

STAN changes the subject.

                    STAN
So you like football then?

                    JAMIE
Love it. It's my dream. Your mate Tom came
to see me play once.
            (beat)

                    JAMIE (CONT'D)
I've got a game on tomorrow. Don't s'pose
you'd like to...?

STAN smiles at him.

                                        FADE TO BLACK.

INT. COCKTAIL BAR - EVENING

MARK ALLEN is with a group of friends. He watches unashamedly as a pretty
WAITRESS 1 threads her way through the tables. He catches her eye and smiles,
she looks away embarrassed. He says something quietly to the other men, they
laugh loudly. She looks over again. MARK signals her.

                    WAITRESS
          1 (Approaching)
Can I help you sir.

                    MARK
What do you reckon guys, can she help
us!

                    MARK'S FRIEND
She can help me, anytime.

The group laugh again. The Waitress 1 smiles tightly at Allen, then glares at them. They stop smiling... they're chicken when confronted! She turns back to Allen.

                    WAITRESS 1
What can I get you?

                    MARK
I'm Mark Allen... the footballer.

The WAITRESS 1 looks blankly at him.

                    WAITRESS 1
So.

                    MARK
So sit down, I'd like to buy you a drink.

                    WAITRESS 1
No thanks.

                    MARK
I don't think you know who I am.

                    WAITRESS
          1 (Mimicking him)
You're Mark Allen... the
footballer.

He grabs her arm, she is alarmed.

                    MARK
Yeah, and I asked you to sit down.

A DOORMAN glances over and she pulls her arm away. She rubs it as she speaks.

                    WAITRESS
Look, what makes you think you can act like

that just cause you're a bit handy with your
right foot?

> MARK
>
> Not just my right foot, darling.

> WAITRESS 1
>
> My little brother idolizes you! He should see
> you now.

She slams the bill down in front of him.

> WAITRESS 1 (CONT'D) And
> guess what? I don't care who you are. All I
> care about is the fact that you're leaving.

She nods to the bouncer to remove them. On the way, MARK pulls out a picture of
himself, signs it and hands it to her.

> MARK
>
> Here. That's for your brother.

She tears it up. MARK and his hangers on are gob smacked.

FADE TO:

INT. CAROL'S FLAT - EVENING

AMOS is home. His hospital bag is on the floor and CAROL is getting him
comfortable. Her eye's are puffy and it is obvious that she's done a lot of
crying.

> AM
> OS (Gently)
> You want to tell me what's up?

> CAR
> OL (sighs)
> It's Jamie.

> AMOS
>
> We've talked about this, love.
> You've got to give him some space.
> He needs time to adjust.

> CAROL
>
> I am.
>   (she sighs)
> I'm scared to say anything anymore.

Everything just seems to upset him. Last night
we had a row he called you a...
          (can't bring herself to say the
            words)
Amos, I slapped him.

AMOS doesn't say anything.

                    CAROL (CONT'D)
Truth be known, I'm ashamed of him.

                    AMOS
It can't be easy for him.

                    CAROL
How can you be so understanding?

                    AMOS
I've got a pretty good idea of what he might
be going through.
          (beat)
Trust me, it takes a strong
character to deal with it.

INT. CAROL'S FLAT - NIGHT

Jamie looks down the corridor towards his CAROL and AMOS bedroom door.
He enters his bedroom and closes door. Music goes on.

                                        FADE TO:

INT. CLASSROOM - DAY

PETER, watched by JAMIE is trying to take the scarf off of a Moslem girl's head.
The Teacher calls PETER out. He argues so she sends him out of the room.
JAMIE gives him the Allen salute which he returns.

                    JAMIE
          (whispering to PETER)
Allen! Allen!

                    PET
          ER (louder)
Allen! Allen!

The teacher looks in hopeless disgust.

EXT. FOOTBALL GROUND - ANOTHER DAY

A game reaches it's climax as JAMIE scores the winning goal. STAN is watching from the touch line in the middle of all the drunken fathers smiling as JAMIE'S team mates celebrate in various styles. The smile fades as he watches JAMIE running round the pitch is encouraged to do the Allen Salute. Stan shakes his head and turns to walk away. JAMIE sees this and realizes that he's let Stan down. He looks sad.

FADE TO:

EXT. STREET - EVENING

STAN shows JAMIE how to dribble a ball properly.

                    STAN
          What about your Mum. Does she ever watch
          you play?

                    JAMIE
          She used to when I was smaller, but now she
          won't come without Amos.

                    STAN
          Amos?

                    JAMIE
          He lives with Mum now.

                    STAN
          And he doesn't like football?

                    JAMI
             E (Shrugs)
          I don't know. He might but...

Stan holds the ball still beneath his foot and waits for Jamie to continue.

                    JAMIE   (CONT'D)
             (looks   around   like   he
             might be overheard)
          He's... black!

                    STAN
          Right?

STAN dribbles off with the ball, leaving JAMIE looking after him. He approaches a small group of drunken father's who had been at the football match and expertly dribbles the ball between them. The Father's can't see STAN only the

ball.

                    FATHER 1
          What the f....?

                  WILL'S FATHER
            (Nodding towards Jamie)
          Bloody voodoo! You've seen his father!

JAMIE looks directly at STAN who regards WILL's FATHER as he staggers off
with the others.

                    JAMIE
          Now do you get it.

STAN thinks deeply as JAMIE departs.

                                            FADE TO:

INT. CAROL'S FLAT - EVENING

CAROL and AMOS are sitting at the kitchen table holding hands as they talk
intimately.

                    CAROL
          I'm not sure we should have left
          London.

                    AMOS
          Is that all you're not sure about?

                    CAROL
          What do you mean?

                    AMOS
          I mean us.
            (beat)
          Stoke isn't the only change.
            (MORE)

                  AMOS (CONT'D)
          At best I could have only been a shadow in
          Jamie's life once upon a time and suddenly
          I'm married to his mum!

CAROL is silent, unsure of how to respond or even if she can. She squeezes AMOS'
hand tighter.

                    CAROL
          Am I less than a mum because the man I've

come to love is not his father? As far as I'm concerned his real father doesn't deserve the title.

AMOS smiles. He pulls her close and kisses her.

> AMOS
> Of course there is always the chance that he might think that you've fallen prey to racial stereotypes and that you are driven by nothing but lust in your pursuit of me!

He grins broadly. CAROL laughs out loud.

> CAROL
> Is that so...

She straddles him, he winces from the pressure of her body on his bruises.

> AMOS
> Ouch! Watch the beat up old man!

They laugh together. They caress. She kisses him passionately.

> CAROL
> Amos. I've never felt like this about anyone before and I'm scared because I think Jamie can see that. And if he does...

JAMIE enters, glances at them, shows disgust then leaves rapidly before they can even say hello.

> CAROL (CONT'D)
> Jamie!

She moves to get up, AMOS holds her back. He calms her with continued caresses

> CAROL (CONT'D)
> (confused, yet resigned)
> What can I do? What they did to you frightened me. We've been friends for a long while but I feel like I've just found you. Really found you.
> (beat)
> I don't want to loose you.

> AMOS
> You'll never loose me.

CAROL smiles briefly, then frowns.

                        CAROL
            But I don't want to loose him either. And
            since the wedding...
            well it's almost like he thinks I've
            stopped loving him.

                        AMOS
            Clearly he does.

CAROL is shocked at his frankness.

                        AMOS
            (CONT'D) You will lose him...
                        (beat)
            ...but only for a while. Love always
            wins out in the end.

CAROL begins to cry.

                        AMOS (CONT'D)
            He'll come back. I promise.

CAROL hugs him. AMOS winces in pain but she doesn't see.

                                        FADE TO:

INT. CAROL'S FLAT - EVENING

JAMIE is lying on the settee. He's thumbing through some of the stuff about Stan.
AMOS enters. He looks in earnest at JAMIE who doesn't look up. AMOS sits in the
chair opposite.

                        AMOS
            Can we talk?

JAMIE doesn't reply

                        AMOS (CONT'D)
            I was thinking about going to see
            Tom's daughter.

JAMIE throws him a sharp glance.

                        AMOS (CONT'D)
            I thought she might let us take the dog out
            every now and again. Would you like that?

                        JAMIE
            S'pose.

                    AMOS (CONT'D)
Okay.

AMOS stands, disappointed in JAMIE'S reaction. As he goes, he spots Stan's face on the front of one of the magazines.

                    AMOS (CONT'D)
Ah, the black man with the white face.

                    JAMIE
What?

                    AMOS
Stanley Matthews... 'the black man with the white face'. That's what we used to call him in Soweto.

                    JAMIE
Where?

                    AMOS
Soweto, in South Africa. He came every summer for twenty five years and taught us kids in the townships how to play his 'beautiful game'.

JAMIE is surprised.

                    AMOS
                    (CONT'D)
                    (Enthusiastically)
He's the reason an African team will win the World Cup one day!

                    JAMIE
In your dreams!

                    AMOS
Maybe. But if... no... WHEN it happens it will be because Stan Matthews planted the seed.

JAMIE resents AMOS knowing so much about Stan. But AMOS realises that he has JAMIE'S attention and sits gingerly on the edge of the sofa as he continues to reminisce.

                    AMOS (V.O.) (CONT'D) It
was really brave of him you
know. Then, we were persecuted in our own

country because our skin was black. Because
of this the rest of the world banned all
sporting contacts with South Africa
            (beat)
Stan thought it was wrong... so he taught
black kids how to beat the whites at their
own game.

This last remark brings a strong facial reaction from JAMIE.

> JAMIE [SARCASTICALLY] How
come you know so much about it then ?

> AMOS
> (His attention back on
> JAMIE)
'Cause I was one of those black kids!

There is silence as JAMIE takes this. Perhaps he begins seeing AMOS with
new eyes. AMOS begins to leave.

> JAMIE
South Africa wouldn't beat England you
know.

> AMOS (exiting,
> smiling.)
Maybe not yet... but Nigeria or
Cameroon?

FADE TO:

INT. CAROL'S FLAT/JAMIE'S BEDROOM - AFTERNOON

JAMIE and STAN are talking.

> JAMIE
Tom told me a lot of amazing stuff about
what you did. Was it true?

> STAN
He wasn't the sort of man to lie. (ponders)
Its not so amazing when you're living it
somehow. But when I look back I was lucky.
Seem to have made a good number of people
happy in my time.

> JAMIE
Yeah, Tom said that sort of stuff lasts in

peoples memories for ever.

>   STAN
> Football can achieve amazing things Jamie.
> When it's played right it can bring people
> together... or separate them, if not!

A pause. JAMIE studies his feet. STAN studies JAMIE

>   JAMI
> E Would you...
>   (looking up and searching
>   STAN'S face)
> ...show me?

>   STAN
> Show you?

>   JAMI
> E Yeah. You know.
>   (beat)
> How to do it right.

STAN nods with a smile. JAMIE'S shell shows signs of cracking at last.

                                        FADE OUT:

MONTAGE SEQUENCE...

EXT. FOOTBALL GROUND - DAY

STAN training JAMIE. Some bemused faces with onlookers as JAMIE
responds to unseen instructions.

>   STAN
> Enthusiasm is the key to success in
> everything.

INT. CAROL'S FLAT - DAY

MONTAGE. Stan inspecting the kitchen and food in the fridge and cupboards.

>   STAN
> It was taking care of my diet that kept me
> playing so long. I fasted every Monday. And if
> I had a particularly difficult game coming up I
> would fast the week before it.

EXT. VICTORIA GROUND - DAY

JAMIE practices the 'Matthews Swerve' and manages to trip himself up and twist his ankle. STAN makes him take his shoe off and performs reflexology on his foot.

> STAN
> My beautiful wife, Mila, taught me how to do
> this.

EXT. CAROLS FLAT - DAY

JAMIE sits on the doorstep with his trainers off. STAN puts a lead weight in each shoe then hands them back to JAMIE who puts them on and ties to run.

> STAN
> I used to walk to the match wearing lead
> weights in my shoes. When I ran out on the
> pitch in ordinary boots, I felt like I was flying.

> FADE OUT MONTAGE
> SEQUENCE:

INT. CAROL'S FLAT - MORNING

CAROL is having a healthy breakfast. JAMIE enters drowsily, goes to the fridge and pulls out a carton of carrot juice. He sits down at the table and pours out a pint of juice.

> CAROL
> Go easy on that love. You don't want to be
> turning orange do you?

> JAMIE
> Mum.

> CAROL
> Yes?

> JAMIE
> We ever been to Blackpool?

> CAROL
> Once when you were really young, (beat)
> You wouldn't remember .

> JAMIE
> Could we go again?

                              CAROL
                 I suppose so. Can I ask why?

                              JAMI
                 E I thought...
                         (beat)
                 ...it would be, interesting.

AMOS enters.

                              CAROL
                 Why don't you ask Amos?

                              AMOS
                 Ask me what?

Silence as CAROL looks at JAMIE - but JAMIE clearly has no intention of
asking.

                              CAROL
                 Jamie wants you to take us to
                 Blackpool.

JAMIE stares daggers. AMOS is reticent and exchanges glances with CAROL. But
she gives him 'a look'.

                              AMOS
                 (somewhat reluctantly) Oh,
                 okay. I'll do it.

Both AMOS and JAMIE look uncomfortable.

BLACKPOOL PROMENADE - DAY

They are driving along the golden mile when suddenly a gang of skinhead
England supporters in England shirts spill into the road ahead. AMOS overreacts
and brakes sharply. A cyclist nearly runs into the back of them. He curses and the
Skinheads turn around and stare into the car. AMOS has stalled. He quickly
restarts it, moving away sharply. JAMIE watches the departing scene through the
rear window. The dumbest of the skinheads wears a Mark Allen T-shirt and does
the salute. Jamie begins to doubt a little as AMOS breathes a deep sigh of relief.

                              AMOS
                 Okay. Where to? The tower,
                 pleasure beach, water park?

                              JAMIE
                 Bloomfield Road!

                    CAROL
Where?

                    AMOS
Blackpool FC... where Stanley
Matthews once played.

AMOS gives CAROL a 'don't ask' look and she decides to leave it alone.

BLACKPOOL FC - DAY

They drive round Bloomfield Road. Inside the car JAMIE is looking out at the
name "Blackpool FC. After one circuit AMOS stops the car.

                    AMOS
Do you want to get out to see if you can find
whatever it is you're looking for?

                    JAMIE
Okay.

He gets out of the car, smiles as he looks ahead. He approaches the entrance to
Blackpool FC offices. Everywhere there are images of Stan and the 1953 team. He
peers through the glass doors. The desk is empty. STAN is on the stairs and he
beckons to him. He follows him up the stairs.

INT. STAN MATTHEWS' SUITE. - DAY

They look out over the ground outside where AMOS and CAROL are idly
looking around until JAMIE returns.

                    STAN
So that's Amos is it? He looks familiar.

                    JAMIE
They all look the same if you ask me.

STAN looks at him.

                    JAMIE (CONT'D)
What?
        (tuts realising what he's said)
Sorry, I didn't mean that. (beat)
I am trying to get to grips with it, but it's
not easy you know.

                    STAN
What?

                    JAMIE
A black man with my mum!

                    STAN
What if Amos were white but ten years older
than her, how would you feel then?

                    JAMIE
        (beat)
I wouldn't like it, but he's...

                    STAN
Really? And where does 'love' come into this
equation?

JAMIE rolls his eyes.

                    STAN (CONT'D)
Okay, it doesn't mean anything much at your
age but when you reach my age...

                    JAMIE
Stan, you died ten years ago! Even you aren't
your age.

STAN laughs.

                    STAN
        (Suddenly serious)
Love is very real. It can enter your life in
the most unexpected form and it really
doesn't recognise borders.

                    MATURE JAMIE.
Then what he told me I will never, ever
forget!

JAMIE is struck by the sincerity in STAN's words. He listens closely, his cynicism
suddenly dispelled.

                    STAN:
Look, when I was fifty three I was managing
Port Vale for free. I took the team to
Czechoslovakia. We were assigned a really
lovely and sophisticated young woman as
our cultural guide. I don't know how it
happened, anyone would've told you I'm not
a ladies' man – and she was thirteen years
younger than me – but we fell in love.

STAN is staring fixedly at the pitch which becomes a green screen, against

which the love story is played out.

                    STAN
     It was 1968, everything was changing. Love
     was everywhere and anything was possible!
     So I went back to Prague to be with her and
     then suddenly, something happened to make
     me realize that the world hadn't changed as
     much as everyone had thought. The Russians
     invaded! I came out on the last train. I went
     home and it tore me apart. Mila was still
     there. There I was, back in Blackpool, Sir
     Stanley Matthews - the first footballing
     Knight, the first European footballer of the
     year, a role model to millions of people. And
     yet here I was – wanting to quit my marriage -
     everything - for a married woman thirteen
     years younger than me who filled my heart
     completely. Suddenly I got a call – she was out
     and in Germany. Within days I was with her.
                    (MORE)

                    STAN (CONT'D)
     We spent the next seven years dodging the
     press, hiding our love from the wide world
     when all I wanted to do was to shout it out!
          (beat)
     I was as proud of my love in her as anything I
     achieved in football.

STAN goes quiet. But JAMIE is impatient to know more.

                    JAMIE:
     But what happened?

STAN jolts back from his memories.

                    STAN:
     My divorce came through... after seven
     years.

                    JAMIE:
     And?

                    STAN:
     And... eventually... we were able to come
     back to Stoke, and live openly, honestly... as
     husband and wife.
          (beat)
     So you see, I've been there. I know exactly
     what your mum and Amos are going through.

INT. AMOS' CAR / EXT. BLACKPOOL FC -- DAY

AMOS is lazily checking his rear view mirror as he and CAROL wait. JAMIE suddenly appears looking pleased. He climbs into the car.

                    AMOS
          You done already?

                    JAMIE
          Yes.
                    (beat)
          Thanks.

AMOS and CAROL look shocked... JAMIE said 'thanks' to AMOS? As they look quizzically at each other, JAMIE spots a 'Kick Racism poster' in the window of the Sales office.

                    JAMIE (CONT'D)
          Mum. Have you got a couple of quid
          I can borrow.

AMOS reaches into his pocket.

                    AMOS
          There you go.

                    JAMIE
          Thanks.

AMOS and CAROL mouth 'thanks' to each other as he says it again. JAMIE meanwhile walks towards the shop.

EXT SHOP - DAY

Jamie emerges wearing a wristband. More shocks all round!

                                                  FADE TO:

EXT. ST.ANNE'S BEACH - MORNING

STAN in a track suit with a flat cap. JAMIE and STAN are running together. Stan pulls up JAMIE keeps going.

                    ST
          AN
                    (Shouting)
          Come back. What have I told you?

                        JAMIE
Oooops!

                        STAN
Just short sprints.

                        JAMIE
Sorry.

                        STAN
You only need to be super fast over seven or
eight yards. By then your opponent is left for
dead.

                        JAMIE
Okay.

He starts to jog.

                        STAN
        Hold on!

JAMIE looks round.

                    STAN (CONT'D)
        Just walk a bit. Take some time for you.

They walk together. JAMIE goes to speak then sees Stan's gaze is fixed out to
sea.

                    STAN (CONT'D)
        I love this place.
                (thoughtful)
        What do you see out there?

JAMIE is uncertain what to say. He scans the horizon for ships or birds.

                        JAMIE
        I can't see anything, just the sea.

                        STAN
Just the sea?

JAMIE scrutinises STAN'S face, then the sea.

                    STAN (CONT'D) Sometimes
in the mornings the sea mists are so thick I
wouldn't be able to see you walking there.
Then you really are alone. The

person I've always tried to be, the Stan
Matthews the world thinks it knew dissolves
and I'm alone with the real me.
>   (beat)
Go!

They sprint again and pull up. STAN'S eyes are distant. JAMIE is
unsettled.

>   JAMIE
>   Sounds weird... scary.

STAN smiles.

>   STAN
>   Always remember Jamie, what's outside is
>   temporarily... but what's inside never is. The
>   really scary stuff is what we create outside...
>   or others create for us and expect us to live
>   up to.

>   JAMIE
>   But everyone wants to be famous, that's
>   good isn't it?

>   STAN
>   Is it?

CAROL and AMOS walk over to JAMIE from the prom as Stan barks out again.

>   STAN (CONT'D)
>   Go!

They sprint again down the beach. AMOS speaks.

>   AMOS
>   Fancy a kick about?

STAN stands next to AMOS, looking at JAMIE. This is a big decision for him.

>   JAMIE
>   What about your injuries?

>   AMOS
>   I'll go in goal.

He peels off his top and throw it down for a goalpost. As he does so a group of
white women [from Liverpool?] whistle and catcall admiration. JAMIE is flustered
by this but eventually does likewise. The girls catcall again delighting in his
embarrassment.

                    JAMIE
          OK.

                    AMOS
               (smiling broadly)
          Alright!

STAN smiles and wanders a short distance away before sitting down and
watching them play. CAROL smiles.

EXT. BLACKPOOL PROMENADE [SQUIRES GATE] - DAY

CAROL passes close by the women holding drinks she's just gotten for her
two men.

                    WOMAN
          They belong to you?

                    CAROL
          My son and my husband.

                    WOMAN

          Lucky girl!

                    CAROL
          Thank you.

CAROL smiles proudly as she watches her men play.

                                                        FADE TO:

INT. CAROL'S FLAT - EVENING

AMOS opens the door and lets CAROL and JAMIE pass. They carry their bags from
the trip in. A local paper lies on the mat.

                    CAROL
          Pick that up will you, love.

AMOS picks up the paper and reads. MARK ALLEN is all over the front page. The
picture shows him attacking another player. The headline screams, 'The Ugly face
of the beautiful Game'. He sighs and hands it to JAMIE frowns and tosses the
paper away dismissively before heading to his room.

                    JAMIE
          Thanks mum and... dad. I had a great
          trip!

CAROL and AMOS stare at each other, jaws dropped wide open.

INT. CAROL'S BEDROOM - NIGHT

CAROL is in bed. AMOS is undressing. She eyes his body with pleasure. Amos, stiff with pain and his healing injuries, lies carefully on bed. Carol begins to massage his injuries.

> AMOS
> (reflectively)
> Do you know what that boy has in the
> cases in his room?

> CAROL
> (Distractedly)
> No.

She runs her hands over his body back and massages.

> AMOS
> It's full of paper-cuttings and
> programmes, books and magazines. All
> about one man... Stanley Matthews.

> CAROL
> Should I be worried?

AMOS moves close to her.

> AMOS
> No. He's one influence I definitely wouldn't
> mind him coming under.

He kisses her. She seems assured. He slowly caresses her skin.

> AMOS (CONT'D)
> You know, I saw Tom's daughter the other
> day.

> CAROL
> (somewhat distracted by the
>   caressing)
> Oh yes, how is she?

> AMOS
> Not good I'm afraid. She's said they're
> going to have to give Laddie up, cause
> they're out at work all day.

                          CAROL
          Where's he gonna go.

                          AMOS
          Well, he's to old to re-home, so it seems
          they'll have to put him down.

                          CAROL
          That's dreadful.

                          AMOS
          Yes.
                    (beat)
          So I'm wondering if we take him...
          for Jamie. I know we're in a flat but the
          dog's old and it might be really good for
          the boy to have some responsibility for
          once.
                    (then, kissing her gently) What
          do you reckon?

                          CAROL
          Oh, I don't know...

AMOS kisses here more passionately and stares into her eyes.

                          AMOS
          Just for me?

She smiles... won over by passion.

                          CAROL
          Oh... alright!

AMOS smiles and switches the light off as they embrace.

                                        FADE TO:

EXT. CAROL'S FLAT - NEXT DAY

AMOS is waiting in the car, the engine running. CAROL, outside the car
calls out to JAMIE inside the house.

                          CAROL
          Jamie! A friend's come to see you!

JAMIE exits, wondering what on earth she's talking about. Amos opens the
passenger door and the old dog lumbers out towards JAMIE. JAMIE's eyes widen
when he sees him. He picks the dog up and is greeted by a huge sloppy kiss.

                    JAMIE
          Laddie!

                    AMOS
          We thought you might like to have someone
          to keep you company during your practice
          from now on!

JAMIE can't help smiling broadly. CAROL hands him a lead. JAMIE fixes it to
Laddie's collar and they head off along the street. CAROL and AMOS watch,
exchanging smiles.

                    MATURE JAMIE.
          Little did I know at the time but the arrival
          of Tom's old waddling dog marked the
          beginning of my growing up... both inside
          and out!

                                        FADE TO BLACK:

EXT. FOOTBALL STADIUM - EVENING GAME

(Visually parodying the Heidi Riefenstal Nazi propaganda film...)

A game is on. Allen and a black player go for a high ball together. Allen leads
with his elbow. Blood pours from the black player's face as Allen is shown the
red card. He returns to the fallen opponent, shouts abuse at him and stamps
on his ankle. We hear it crack.

The referee and linesman intercede. He spits in their faces. A policeman runs up
to intercede and he strikes out again.

                                        FADE TO:

EXT. WASTE GROUND - DAY

PETER and JAMIE are sitting near a canal. LADDIE is plodding around. Both boys
are skimming stones at a distant object.

                    PETER
          What's up with you?

                    JAMIE
          What d'you mean?

                    PETER
          You've been really strange lately.

JAMIE looks, wondering if somehow he's discovered about Stan.

> PETER (CONT'D)
> It started since after we robbed that old
> bloke. You've not wanted to join in since he
> died.
> (beat)
> Even when you're with us these days...
> you're not there anymore!

JAMIE looks away and skims another stone.

> PETER (CONT'D) Yea,
> just like you are now...
> distant. I tell you, it's put the shit up Will.

> JAMIE
> That figures.

> PETER
> Keeps saying... you're going to drop us in it...
> from a big height.

> JAMIE
> He's a prat!

JAMIE Looks at LADDIE.

> JAMIE (CONT'D)
> He's a racist prat... of the first order!

PETER is totally shocked to hear his friend say that and puzzles over it. JAMIE meanwhile skims a stone hard. It hits its target, which resonates.

> PETER
> What's up with you? You even talk
> different. Where do you get this stuff?

> JAMIE
> Certainly not from Will!

PETER looks quizzically at his friend. JAMIE does dumb zombie gesture of Will. They both laugh. The tension is broken.

> PETER
> I feel sorry for him... with a dad like that.

> JAMIE
> Yeah. He's... we're all... allowing Will's Dad
> and Granddad to set the pattern of our lives.

                    (then, looking at Laddie) And look at
          the harm it causes on the way.

PETER calls LADDIE across and begins to pet the dog who licks him.

                         PETER
          You're beginning to sound like my
          granddad. And if Will could hear you he'd
          be shitting himself even harder.

                         JAMIE
          Yeah, well I ain't scared of him anymore.

                                        FADE TO BLACK.

EXT. VICTORIA GROUND - DAY

JAMIE and STAN are kicking a ball about, then take a break from training.

                         STAN
          I've something I'd like to tell you and then I
          have a favour to ask.

JAMIE looks questioningly in response.

                         STAN (CONT'D)
          When my father was dying, he asked two
          things of me, one of which was easy. To look
          after my mum. The second proved a good
          deal harder.

STAN'S mind drifts back JAMIE is all ears.

                         JAMIE
          What was it?

                         STAN (V.O.)
                 (mischievously)
          To win the FA Cup!

(Flash back: Simulated footage of the 1953 Final. STAN is on the pitch afterwards
holding his medal up to the sky.)

                         STAN
          Happily for me and for him both happened.
          That medal was for Dad. I knew somehow
          he'd rest easier after that.

Back to present day.

                    JAMIE
But you said he died years before that?

                    STAN
That's true. But a dying wish unfulfilled
somehow has a hold on the dead... and the
living. So what I'm going to ask you now are
two very special favours of my own.

STAN demonstrates kicking a ball expertly. He indicates JAMIE should copy him
and JAMIE does so with the real ball. They walk to retrieve it.

                    STAN (CONT'D)
When my Mili died, it was very sudden. I was
away in hospital having a check up. She had a
heart attack watching the telly. I'd always told
her to give up smoking.
          (beat to reminisce)
She loved her garden, the original 'green
fingers' she was.
          (clears the lump in his
            throat)

                    STAN (CONT'D)
Anyway, she'd been on at me for ages to put
up this bird table she bought and I hadn't
done it. When she went I gave up the will to
live, let alone put up a bird table. But you
know... that was my dying regret.

They arrive at the ball. STAN looks at JAMIE who's beginning to get a glimmer of
understanding of what he's getting at.

                    STAN (CONT'D)
A Begonia at the base would be a lovely
finishing touch.
          (beat)
She loved them.

                    JAMIE
Let me get this straight. You want me to put
up a bird table and plant flowers...

                    STAN
Begonia's!

                    JAMIE
Begonias, in someone else's garden?

                    STAN
That's it. At least that's the first thing!

JAMIE picks up the ball, lobs it up and hoofs it into the distance. He looks at STAN quizzically.

                    JAMIE
               (exaggerated speculation)
          Let me guess the second. You want me to
          break into Stoke City and retrieve your
          ashes from under the Centre spot.

                    STAN
               (Deadpan, going along with it)
          Only half of them. The rest are in the garden
          with Mila's.

                    JAMIE
          But, I'd get into trouble! I'll be arrested and...
          so will Amos!

A broad grin suddenly breaks out on STAN'S face. He has successfully been winding JAMIE up.

                    STAN
          No. The second wish is a lot more difficult
          than that, son!

                                        FADE TO BLACK...

EXT. THE VIEWS {STAN'S LAST HOUSE] - NIGHT

JAMIE is digging around in the ground under cover of night carrying out his promise to Stan. He is unaware that a man giving his dog a late night run sees him. The man watches for a few minutes before hurrying quietly off. JAMIE Puts the finishing touches to his chore, packs his tools away in a hold all and hurries out of the garden. Mission accomplished. He heads off up the little road that leads to the house.

                                        FADE TO:

EXT. JAMIE'S HOUSE - LATER

A Police car is parked nearby, lights off. As JAMIE approaches the two officers get out of the car. A torch is shone into his face and his heart drops. Busted again!

                                        FADE TO:

INT. STOKE POLICE STATION - NIGHT

AMOS walks into the station. He approaches the front desk and comes face to face with the same officer who cautioned JAMIE before in Leeds.

                    SERGEANT
          We meet again Mr. Matkoni!

                    AMOS
          Goodness!
                    (recovering well)
          I thought you were based in Leeds?

                    SERGEANT
          Transfer, sir. First day today. It's always nice
          to see a familiar face on your first day, don't
          you think.

                    AMOS
          What's he charged with this time?

                    SERGEANT
          Trespass and theft.

                    AMOS
          Theft?

                    SERGEANT
          That's right, Sir. He was caught red handed
          with his bag full of gardening tools.

Out on AMOS lost for words.

                                        FADE TO:

EXT. 1 THE VIEWS - MORNING

An elderly couple look in amazement at the bird table planted in the middle of the lawn. The old lady notices a golden plaque on it.

                    OLD LADY
          What does that say, dear?

                    OLD MAN
          For Mila!

                                        FADE TO:

EXT. FOOTBALL GROUND - AFTERNOON

A football match is in play. JAMIE is playing well. The other FATHER'S are all along the touchline, drinking and loudmouthed as usual. To one side STAN directing Jamie enthusiastically. AMOS' car pulls in near the pitch.

INT. AMOS CAR - SAME MOMENT.

                        AMOS

(Turning to CAROL)
            You ready for this?

                        CAROL
            Are you?

AMOS nods and gets out of the car. He goes round the other side and opens the door for CAROL.

                        CAROL (CONT'D)
            Thank you kind sir.

EXT. FOOTBALL GROUND - SAME MOMENT.

CAROL takes AMOS' arm and they walk huddled close together towards the match. As they get closer there are various remarks from the FATHERS. Nevertheless, they join the crowd, remaining slightly distanced at one end.

                        WILL'S FATHER (to
                    WILL, nearby on the pitch)
            That weirdo mate of yours... I don't want you
            hanging out with him anymore, you hear?

Smacks him round the head for good measure as he passes.

                        WILL
                    (then, shouting to JAMIE)
            Hey black boy. You're Dad's here.

JAMIE looks. He starts to react when STAN catches his eye. STAN is shaking his head and mouthing "No Fuss. Ignore him." JAMIE acknowledges. JAMIE answers by doing a brilliant move. The barracking of JAMIE, CAROL and AMOS increases as the touchline FATHER's swig more from their cans. JAMIE is clouted by WILL as they go for a ball together. JAMIE stays down a little while. WILL with a grin on his face scoffs silently. JAMIE stands and faces him with a glare.

                        JAMIE
                    (scarily strong)
            Don't EVER do that to me again Will!

You hear?

WILL buckles and looks sheepishly to his dad, who scowls at him for being such a wimp. He leads the other fathers away, disgusted with his son. JAMIE meanwhile plays a blinder. STAN looks pleased. As the whistle blows as stranger walks towards CAROL and AMOS.

>   JIMMY
>   You're Jamie's parents I believe?

He offers his hand.

>   JIMMY (CONT'D)
>   I'm with the Stan Matthews
>   Foundation. I'd like to talk to you about
>   involving Jamie in what we're doing. As I'm
>   sure you're aware He's head and shoulders
>   above these other lads.
>   (MORE)

>   JIMMY (CONT'D)
>   (beat)
>   Can we chat?

CAROL and AMOS agree and their dialogue fades as they walk.

EXT. FA HEADQUARTERS - TV SCREEN IMAGE

MARK ALLEN wearing dark glasses is being ushered into a car. Camera's flash, microphones are thrust in his direction and voices call out for his attention. Journalists shout out things like 'Mark, over here'. 'What do you think of the ban'

>   REPORT
>   ER (TO
>   CAMERA)
>   Today the FA took the unprecedented step of
>   banning the England International Mark Allen
>   for twenty eight games. The ban was for Allen
>   bringing the game into disrepute for
>   deliberately breaking the leg of fellow
>   International(INSERT NAME)by stamping on
>   it in the ugly race-motivated incident that has
>   shocked even the football world. We
>   understand the Police are also considering
>   charges of grievous bodily harm and racist
>   assault.

INT. JAMIE'S BEDROOM - DAY

The camera pulls back to reveal the news report was on a small portable television that's in the corner of Jamie's room. STAN and JAMIE have been watching.

                    STAN
          That's the end of his England career!
                    (then, with a twinkle in his
                      eye)
          Perhaps I should make a comeback?

                    JAMIE
          If only.

JAMIE leafs through his STAN memorabilia.

                    JAMIE (CONT'D)
                    (Enthralled)
          Tell me about the nineteen fifty three Cup
          Final.

                    STAN
          I was thirty eight. I already had two losers
          medals and everyone was saying it was my
          last chance to get a winners medal. Good
          wishes came from all over the world. It was
          actually the first Final to be televised. I think
          the whole country stopped at the time.

JAMIE fondles the 1953 programme.

                    STAN (CONT'D)
          There was no way we were going to lose.
          Although, for a long time, I thought otherwise.

Recreate black and white footage of the game as STAN talks over.

                    STAN (V.O.)
          At half time we were two one down Their
          Fullback, Bell had been badly injured and
          there were no substitutes in those days, so
          they moved him onto the wing and blow me,
          just after the restart - he scores. Stan
          Mortensen pulled back a goal from my cross,
          then hit an incredible free kick with two
          minutes to go. The atmosphere was fantastic
          and so was what happened next. Our inside
          right put a beautiful pass to the edge of the
          box. I was onto it quickly, I took it inside and

was looking for Morty. I panicked a bit, went
to the right of the defender. Morty was going
for the near post, drawing players onto him,
but he had shouted to Bill Perry to fill in
behind. It was the simplest of passes and I
slipped making it. The next day in all the
papers it was hailed as the 'Matthews final'
and has remained so ever since.

End retro footage.

                    STAN
          I have always been embarrassed by that. How
          can another man score a hat trick in a Cup
          Final and yet it forever be known as my
          game?

                    JAMIE
          I guess the crowd loved you the most
Stan!

JAMIE looks up at his Mark Allen poster. He gets up, goes to it and takes it down.

                    JAMIE (CONT'D)
          Amos told me what you did for the
          South Africans.

                    STAN
          Ay. There were some really good
          players there.

A knock at the door. AMOS pokes his head round the door. He sees the poster
coming down.

                    AMOS
          You're mums been slaving over a hot oven
          and has produced a feast. You hungry?

                    JAMIE
              (with a genuine smile) You
bet!

                                        FADE TO:

EXT. STOKE FOOTBALL GROUND - DAY

AMOS drives up outside the Stoke ground. JAMIE is next to him with CAROL
in the back. She leans forward and surreptitiously kisses JAMIE on the cheek.

CAROL

Good luck!

JAMIE smiles. AMOS offers a high five.

AMOS

Yea, good luck son...
[beat]
...as if you need it!

JAMIE takes the hand briefly, then opens the door. As he turns to close it he
leans in to AMOS.

JAMIE

You really do love her don't you?

AMOS

Never a doubt.
(beat)
...from the very first.

Smiles all round. JAMIE turns and walks towards STAN, who is standing beside
his own statue. Amos exits the car and catches up with him.

AMOS (CONT'D)

There's something else that man...
(pointing to the shadow)
...did for people like me. (beat)
He stopped us becoming anti white!

JAMIE

What?
(beat)
Why?

AMOS

Because we were able to say to ourselves
that there are white people who care about
our plight. Stanley Matthews, the most
famous footballer in the world, did that by
simply being there with us year after year.
You can't imagine what that meant to us... to
have such a man on our side.

AMOS returns to CAROL and they drive off. Other cars arrive, dropping off their
kids of varying ethnicity. JAMIE studiously examines Stan's statue. STAN is
beside him. To observers, he appears to be talking to himself.

                    JAMIE
              (to STAN)
          You know, I reckon that sculptor got it
          right.

                    STAN
          In what way?

                    JAMIE
          One of your legs really is shorter than the
          other! No wonder you could do that
          Matthew's swerve!

He ducks STAN's clip around the ear and scatters towards the entrance hop-
along style.

                                                      FADE TO:

INT. STANLEY MATTHEWS FOUNDATION / OFFICE -- DAY

JAMIE has been called in and is standing across the desk from BOB, the
Foundation's manager.

                    BOB
          Congratulations Jamie!

JAMIE looks uncertain.

                    JAMIE
          Sir?

                    BOB
          Old Tom did us a real favour when he told
          us about you. It might even be that he's
          done the game a favour too. The way
          you've been playing... it could have been
          the great Stan Matthews out there himself!

JAMIE smiles knowingly.

                    BOB (CONT'D)
          Where the heck did you get all those
          moves?

JAMIE struggles for an answer. Luckily BOB continues.

                    BOB (CONT'D)
          I had the Stoke Manager on the phone
          yesterday. He was very impressed. He wants
          to put you in their youth team next season!

A huge grin breaks out on JAMIE'S face.

                    BOB (CONT'D)
          And I kinda hope you'll stick around here too.
          How'd you fancy a summer job here at the
          foundation... coaching other kids.

                    JAMI
               E (Excited)
          Really?

                    BOB
          As you know we're a charity so the money
          won't be huge.

                    JAMIE
          I don't care about the money. This is the best
          day ever!

                    BOB
          Good. Start on Monday then... eh?

                    JAMIE
          Sure! I can't wait to tell Sta...
               (beat)
          Er, I mean mum... and Amos.

He starts to rush out. Bob calls out after him.

                    BOB
          You'll be in charge of the first ever Stan
          Matthews Eleven Girls Team.

JAMIE'S face drops, but fortunately BOB can't see it.

                                        FADE TO:

EXT. STOKE STREETS - MOMENTS LATER

JAMIE is walking fast down the street... and occasional skip and jump showing
his joy. He can't believe what's just happened. STAN'S second request echo's
through his mind.

                    MATURE JAMIE.
          It was then that I remembered
          Stan's second request...

                    STAN
                 (v.o.)
          I want you to pass on everything I've taught
          you about the spirit of the game and doing it
          right. Promise me you'll find a way to do that
          for me.

JAMIE smiles. He reaches into his pocket and pulls out the badge Tom gave him.
He looks at it and then to the heavens.

                    JAMIE
          But they're girls, Stan! Girls!

                                                  FADE TO:

EXT. STOKE FOOTBALL GROUND / PITCH -- DAY

The GIRLS are gathered around JAMIE as he coaches them in Stan's methods.
STAN looks on from the terrace with TOM by his side.

                    JAMIE
          Okay, lets go and remember enthusiasm is
          the key to success.

The GIRLS break out into pairs. JAMIE is showing them how to jockey but he's
having trouble with the feisty and attractive black girl he's picked to demonstrate
with. She is a very skilful player and keeps dribbling the ball around him. Finally
they tumble in a tackle. JAMIE offers his hand, she takes it and he pulls her up.
Their eyes meet. The girl smiles, JAMIE blushes and puts his head down.
Embarrassed he glances at STAN who is with TOM in the stand.

STAN shrugs his shoulders.

                    ST
               AN (to
               TOM)
          This time he's on his own!
               (Shakes his head)
          Football I understand!

They depart, leaving Jamie to deal with things on his own.

                                              FADE TO BLACK...

US CITY STADIUM - MODERN TIMES, AS BEFORE.

Still in ultra slow motion, Jamie stares down the goalkeeper as the ghostly Stan
continues to urge him to kick the ball into the far right-hand corner of the goal.

MATURE JAMIE.
Stan never did leave completely. He had
always told me he would always be there
until he was certain I didn't need him any
more. I was never sure what he meant by that
but I trusted I would know when the time
came. But always did exactly what he told me,
and did it to the letter. But that day, right
then, I had a feeling I had to trust my own
judgement.

Jamie smiles weakly to Stan, then looks to the goal with great
determination.

COMMENTATOR 1
What a moment for Jamie Steele. The
outcome of this game rests entirely on this
kick. Many of the fans or his team mates can't
even watch! Oh boy, oh boy, oh boy!

COMMENTATOR 2
Yea Brian! Talk about tension!

The tension merely increases as Jamie, still moving in ultra slow motion, runs up
towards the ball, about to shoot. Stan still points where he wants Jamie to shoot.
Eventually Jamie kicks the ball hard and firmly. However, instead of directing the
ball towards where Stan had indicated, Jamie fires it instead towards the opposite
end of the goal. The goalkeeper gets it entirely wrong - diving in the direction
where Stan had indicated. Unchallenged, Jamie's shot miraculously curves itself
around the defensive wall and then on towards the goal. The diving goalkeeper
watches helplessly as the ball bends in goalwards. Stan looks surprised too.

CUT TO:

CLOSE UP OF GOAL - SAME MOMENT.

Now suddenly accelerating to real time the ball speeds over the goaline and
smashes into the net at the back.

COMMENTATOR 1
Oh lordie! Have you ever seen anything like
that! The goal of the season - the century - by
the amazing Jamie Steele! Unbelievable!

COMMENTATOR 2
Wow! Did you see the swerve he put on that
ball. I didn't know it was possible. Sign him
up Brazil!

ANNOUNCER 1
He certainly knows how to cap an important
moment in style. Look at those fans go
crazy!

                                                                CUT TO:

WIDE VIEW OF THE END OF THE GROUND - SAME MOMENT.

The Spurs fans are erupting with joy. The City goalkeeper collapses onto the
ground and beats it in total frustration.

The City players slump when they see what has just occurred. Jamie's teammates run towards him with joy. Even Stan looks surprised.

COMMENTATOR 1
What jubilation. And that has to be that!
Surely there's no more time left in this match
now?

COMMENTATOR 2
Yep Brian. That has to be it, surely!

Meanwhile, Jamie's teammates have attempted to crowd around him but he was
to quick and excited to let them. Instead, he zigzagged between everyone and has
run towards Stan. He stands before his mentor, arms outstretched with joy. For a
moment he fears Stan's reaction to his clear disobedience. To tease his protege,
Stan first looks sternly back at Jamie - but then breaks out to a broad grin and
applauds him. (The crowd think that Jamie is standing facing them and cheer
wildly at him of course as they don't see Stan.) Jamie gives Stan a relieved smile.
Stan points to the main stand where Jamie's wife and kids are cheering with
everyone else. Jamie looks and we see his wife is the black girl we had seen when
he was teaching the girl team earlier. She holds onto two beautiful light brown
children who cheer madly for their dad. One proudly wears the Stan badge that
Tom had given Jamie so long ago. Suddenly Jamie is buried under a mound of
excited teammates who have finally caught up with him. Jamie is swept off his
feet as he is carried head-high by his cheering teammates.

COMMENTATOR 1
Oh my, have you ever seen anything like this
folks? History is being made as we watch...
and Jamie Steele yet again weaving his
amazing magic.

COMMENTATOR 2
The most unbelievable soccer moment ever,
Brian?

COMMENTATOR 1
COMMENTATOR 1
I would say so... at least since that magical
'Matthews Final' in the British FA Cup all
those decades ago!

COMMENTATOR
2 (with a playful dig)
That one was a bit before MY time Brian!

                                                    CUT TO:

WIDE VIEW OF THE ENTIRE STADIUM - SHORTLY AFTER.

Meanwhile, the players have returned to the center spot for the kick off. The referee blows the whistle and the match is resumed.

ANNOUNCER 1
And here we go again. How many
seconds left I wonder?

But the minute the ball is kicked off by City the ref immediately blows the whistle to end the game. The stadium erupts once more. Players and coaching staff swarm over Jamie again and once more lift him up onto their shoulders. They carry him towards the fans. Jamie remembers Stan and turns to look where his mentor had been standing.

                                                    CUT TO:

CU JAMIE'S FACE - SAME MOMENT.

Jamie's face suddenly looks disappointed and sad.

                                                    CUT TO:

CU OF CROWD WHERE STAN WAS STANDING - SAME MOMENT.

Stan is gone! Beyond, the fans cheer deliriously as Jamie is carried towards them. But there is no trace of Stan to be seen.

                                                    CUT TO:

MS OF JAMIE ON PLAYER'S SHOULDERS - SAME MOMENT.

Jamie is clearly upset to see that Stan is no longer with him. He smiles philosophically...

                    MATURE JAMIE
And so this was the moment. Stan had said
'when I no longer needed him' he would go...
and I guess this is it. I only hope that one day
I'll be able to thank him properly for
everything he's done for me! In the meantime,
maybe I'll just continue to share his message
about the beautiful game with anyone who
wants to listen!

                                                    CUT TO:

JAMIE AND PLAYERS IN FRONT OF FANS - SAME MOMENT.

This is JAMIE's right of passage moment. He becomes aware of the cheers all
around him and is suddenly carried away by the emotion of it all. As players
acknowledge their excited fans the camera now begins to pull up and away again.

                    MATURE JAMIE.
And so it ends. Stan is in his heaven and all is
well with the world... well almost. I was the
lucky one. WILL on the other hand followed
his father's example and ended-up in prison
for violence and hate crimes. JOE never made
it either. He's been permanently unemployed
since then, as no-one seems able to trust him.
PETER on the other hand was eventually able
to sort himself out and now... like old TOM
before him... is a driver. My driver! We go
everywhere together and he's become the
best friend I've ever had. Well, except for
STAN of course!

A reversal of the opening sequence. Sounds from the stadium fade far away as
we rise up into the heavens again.

                                            FINAL FADE TO
                                            BLACK...

THE END.